COUCHED IN BLOOD

COUCHED IN BLOOD

by

JUDITH L. MITRANI

ISBN: 978-1-80227-226-0 (pbk)
ISBN: 978-1-80227-227-7 (ebk)

CONTENTS

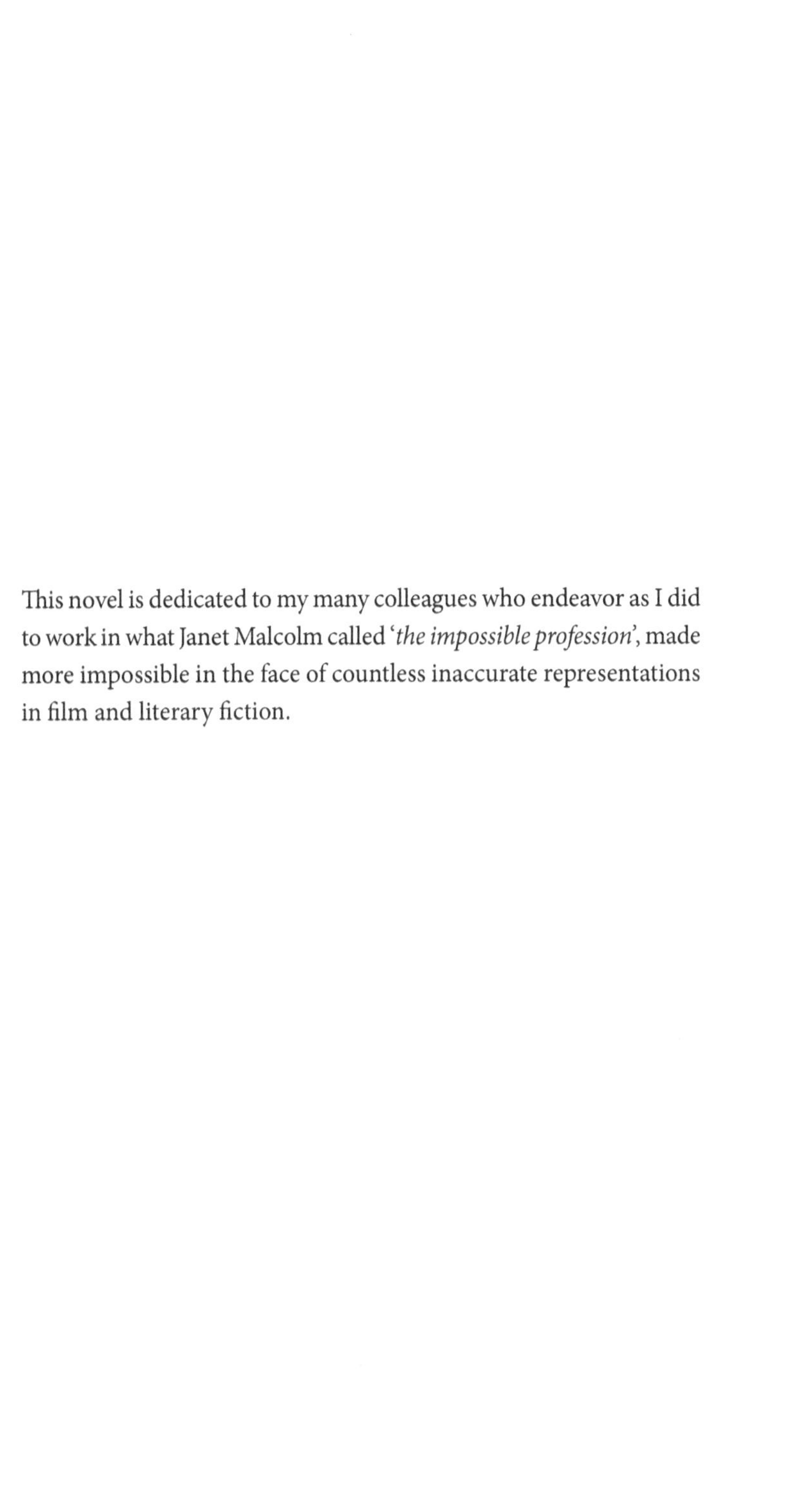
This novel is dedicated to my many colleagues who endeavor as I did to work in what Janet Malcolm called '*the impossible profession*', made more impossible in the face of countless inaccurate representations in film and literary fiction.

PROLOGUE

His face reddened. Veins pulsed as sweat drenched his forehead. He was paralyzed, bleeding thoughts as the light dimmed. *"What the devil is this? Bloody dark! Daylight a moment ago."*

He strained to hold his eyes open. No difference, nothing worked.

"Blast! Can't catch my breath." Something was rising in his chest, burning his throat, flooding his mouth with a hideous metallic taste. His lips trembled, his eyes teared up and overflowed his sunken cheeks.

"Undignified, heart's pounding. Can't hold it. Shit!" He messed himself, lying supine and prostrate, chilled and inwardly struggling. *"Must get up. Ballocks! Can't. Stop this thing. For Christ's sake, stop holding me down."*

Down, down, falling forever. Tied in knots, spilling out, yet heavy as a boulder, dizzy, nauseous, a patchwork of raw sensation yielded a last drop of conscious determination. *"I simply will not abide by this a moment longer. I can't. Stop. Can't stop."*

His inaudible rant faded away on his final word, as all life came to a stop.

She stopped short of reaching for the handle, tapping at the door one last time before entering. Shuddering, she made her way one step at a time across the familiar room where a faint bit of light oozed through the heavily shrouded space. The pool of blood in which the body reposed distinguished itself, little by little, from the sheen of the tufted leather divan. The corpse began to take on an all too familiar shape and stare.

CHAPTER 1

The Final Day

August 1, 1993

Amber rays poured through the west-facing windows of Claudine's room, straining through the narrowed blinds. The light and shadow appeared to impersonate a farm worker, bent over two walls, fingers extending their reach, raking the foot of the couch as if it were a field of hay. Heading into August, the days grew shorter, but this day could not have seemed longer for Claudine. Rachael, a 19-year-old girl, just finishing her first year at university, lay on Claudine's couch. She cried pitifully as she recounted her dream from the previous night.

"Someone handed me a baby dolphin. I thought it could breathe, but I knew that I had to keep putting it in water every so often to keep its skin supple or it would crack open or peel off and the baby dolphin would die in agony. In the dream, I had no place of my own and I kept hopping from one place to another, always other peoples' places. Everywhere I went I tried to find water for the dolphin. I buried my hands in the pockets of my jeans. I was pacing back and forth. I couldn't let it die on my watch."

At first, Claudine felt the words sink like chunks of undigested food, tumbling down into the pit of her stomach. Slowly, Rachael's expressions flowed back up from her body into her mind. Claudine was jolted by the realization of what was the likely impact of Rachael's history. She began to translate, lending significance to the dream. But would her interpretation alter the course of Rachael's experience of what was to come in the long weeks ahead?

"It seems that you are trying to communicate something of what you feel about my summer holiday, about a little you who is very like the baby dolphin in your dream. Maybe a fragile little 'you' who has barely been born, just beginning to breathe the air outside the safety of your place in my room, like a newborn outside Mother's womb. Your dream seems to convey a sense of the danger that you are anticipating as we lose our connection, as you lose contact with this room, with my body, my voice. Perhaps you feel in grave peril of a breach in that fragile skin that barely holds you together, that prevents you from falling apart."

Pausing for a moment, Claudine detected a silence indicating a certain readiness for and receptivity to furthering the extent of their emotional contact. She expressed herself with sensitivity. "Perhaps I leave you in danger of dying, frantic, homeless, with no place of your own, no place in which to breathe safely during this space of time when you are so very aware of your vulnerability, like that of the baby dolphin."

Rachael could only nod, as tears rolled down her cheeks into the crevasses of her neck. As she turned her face to the side, her flaxen hair spread out over the pillow, now soaked with grief. She felt understood by Doctor Ingersoll, touched by her words, by the contact. It was all true, her dread of falling apart, of ceasing to be. Without her analyst's insight to hold her together, she was fearful that she might crack open and the essence of who she had been and who she was becoming would spill out uncontrollably. When Rachael finally spoke, her words were barely audible. They were muffled, as if she were under water.

"I'll miss you," she whimpered. "Is it time to stop now?"

"Yes. We are out of time."

Claudine sighed. Running her hands over her skirt, she rose up from her chair. She was barely able to muster a smile. Rachael sat up, reeling. She clutched her purse close to her body with one hand, as if it could hold her up, and adjusted her oversized tortoise-shell sunglasses and her floppy hat with the other hand, hoping to hide from the eyes of a dangerous world, the one she was forced to face just outside the door of Claudine's room.

Claudine followed the waif-like adolescent to the exit. She realized that Rachael hadn't looked back. Claudine thought she didn't dare, seemingly gripped by a chilling fantasy. Was she afraid that she might deplete and drain this woman whom she loved and needed? Was she scared that her ravenous hunger might render her analyst disappeared forever? Rachael had quickly fled leaving Claudine hoping that she would somehow find the way to reinstate their delicate union come the Fall.

Rachael was Claudine's last patient on that final day before the summer holidays. For Claudine, it was a day filled with reminders of the anguish of separation, the ancient sufferings and wounds that an analyst is compelled to debride, to renew and refresh in the process of a therapeutic transformation. But despite all her hopes for the future, Claudine could only experience the pain of the present. At times like these it seemed that all those aimed-for, mollifying transformations were merely aspects of a theory, speculations, and faint promises in this shadowy moment. Even after all these years, throughout the day before a break, she could be made to feel like a kidnapper, a murderer, a mutilator of small children, helpless to defend themselves. Was she luring each of them into their past, while at the same time abandoning each to relive that past, sometimes all alone?

Before Rachael there was Warren, a man in his sixties. He had recently begun to exhibit a rainbow of talent as an actor, talent he had never previously dared to dream that he possessed, capacities that had been encapsulated deep down inside since early childhood. Warren's mother had been very protective of her husband, keeping the boy and his juvenile glitches and genius outside the door of Father's studio.

"Don't bother your father with that nonsense," she'd warn, as she sent the boy into the woods to walk off any grievances or qualms he may have had. Barred from contact with his paternal protector and confidant, one who might have been able to model a robust manhood for the boy, Warren had created an inner father out of the scant experience he'd had, most of which was molded around self-criticism and inhibition. Over the years after college, he'd disparaged and crossed out so many of his passions that he was left with only the enthusiasm, desires, and needs of others to attend to. Warren called himself "the handy man." On this last day before the summer holidays, he saw Claudine as that mother who obstructs and ousts him, and as that father who is inaccessible yet utterly indispensable.

Earlier that day, Claudine had bid farewell to Rob. A ruggedly handsome man in his mid-forties, Rob had been deserted by his mother just after his second birthday. Until he had embarked upon his analysis a year earlier, he had assuaged his infantile fears by cross-dressing, literally hiding in Mother's skirts. This was Rob's way of sheltering himself from the threats associated with aloneness. His treatment was so new, Claudine suspected he might return to the refuge of his perversion during her absence.

Then there was Eve. She had just given birth to her first child. Now she was suddenly faced not only with her own insecurities as a new mother, but also with the infantile insecurities that overflowed from her baby daughter, insecurities that awakened Eve's own long-buried infantile fears of death, and the horrors of exposure and hunger that dated back to her beginnings as a foundling, who had been discarded in a dumpster in a dark and deserted alley.

Other patients, like Mark the film director, Grace the college professor, and Harriet, a psychiatrist in training to become an analyst, each had their own troubled childhood histories and the current day repetitions of these past events to contend with. Countless memories re-emerged in the passion play being acted out between analyst and patient as a part of the therapeutic process and fulminating around the final day of each term. Claudine struggled to put all she'd felt and observed on that last day into perspective.

Claudine jotted down a few notes, more by way of relieving herself of the enormous pressures building up inside, than in an effort to hang on to the emotions and events of the day, replete with the elemental feelings of the awareness of separateness in infancy; such body-memories often lie unmetabolized in the depths of the psyche, impacting nearly every area of life going forward. No wonder most people shied away from such resolute therapies like psychoanalysis. It must be that most people intuit some warning sign that reads *beyond a certain point in heart and mind, there be dragons.*

Claudine was momentarily reinvigorated as she recognized that Rachael's dolphin dream demonstrated a marked improvement in her mental development. It was testimony to the girl's budding tolerance for her substantial vulnerabilities, and to her growing capacity for the awareness of danger. Claudine recalled dreams reported on the eve of other holidays or weekends, dreams depicting a mere sample of the chaos roiling inside Rachael, and the tip of the icy violence upon which this patient had kept herself afloat in a treacherous sea of loss that threatened to inundate and to drown her.

Claudine tried to remember who had referred to psychoanalysis as the "impossible profession." Sometimes she yearned to soothe, advise, and reassure her patients. She often longed to be loved and to give love in some ordinary and outspoken way. But analysis required abstinence, thought rooted in feeling rather than action taken to avoid feeling. Claudine looked back on her own personal experience out of which her conviction about the analytic work had evolved during her training and in the years beyond. These experiences served to remind her of the fact that action is simply a placebo. At best, it merely constitutes a blank fired at the ghosts of childhood trauma.

Claudine had herself negotiated many painful skirmishes against such ghosts. Countless lopsided truces had been made, only to be broken later. She'd been roughly Rachael's age when she finally engaged in the mother of all wars, her own analysis. Her subsequent liberation had enabled her to reclaim the mental territory that had been invaded, occupied, and even restricted in early childhood. She also recovered the emotional resources that had been annexed by an internal foe as cunning and ruthless as that powerful dictator who had rendered her a refugee from her own life for many years.

CHAPTER 2

Patience and Patients

Ralph Orloff was not easily annoyed. Within the politically thorny, uptight circles in which he moved Ralph had become known for his patience, a useful characteristic for a cop. Time and again he was called upon to be unflappable. Families of victims needed to know where their loved ones were. Were they dead, kidnapped? Who were the monsters? They wanted blood! There was nothing more petrifying than a criminal on the loose in the neighborhood, and people pushed for the immediate arrest of just about anyone. False leads came in by telephone and witnesses barged into the station, each one insisting on their right to speak directly with the officer in charge.

"Don't you have any answers yet? What are you waiting for? We demand to speak with your superior!"

Ambitious politicians, their next election hanging in the balance, required resolution immediately if not sooner. The sensation-hungry press wanted details, information, interviews, photos. In the face of it all, Ralph struggled to resist his own tendency toward impatience, perfectionism, and the pervasive dread of the probability that he would fail the people who depended on him.

His years as Doctor Merrill's patient had helped Ralph to develop the patience to go easier on himself and others. But Merrill had never been late in the past. On the contrary, unlike most Beverly Hills doctors who have a policy of double and triple-booking appointments for the same hour, Merrill started and ended his sessions on the dot, as punctual as a Swiss clock. While other physicians were at the mercy of patients who cancelled at the last minute or sometimes just didn't show up, analyst's charge for sessions reserved in the initial discussion of days and hours for the therapy, whether a patient came or not. This policy served to insure the analyst's livelihood, while instilling a sense of mutual respect for time. This feature of the analytic relationship, what analysts refer to as part of a frame, was both refreshing and essential, especially for a patient like Ralph who always attended his sessions on the sly. No, it wasn't that cops didn't see psychotherapists every so often. Nearly all did at one time or another. But those therapists were counselors, marriage counselors, family counselors, stress counselors, support counselors, career counselors, crisis counselors, even substance abuse counselors. But rarely were they psychoanalysts. Analysts were for real nuts, psychos, hysterical housewives, extreme depressives, and anxious neurotics, but not for cops, especially not for detectives.

Once again, Ralph was an exception. He had read about psychoanalysis and had taken a course on Freud at the University of Buffalo, where he'd been an undergrad. He was utterly fascinated, hooked by the workings of the unconscious, intrigued by his own dreams and the notion of what they might mean. Ah, meaning! The idea that everything has it, even dreams. It was a belief that had appealed to Ralph from the get-go. His dreams became mysteries within mysteries, about all subjects mysterious.

When Ralph approached impatience, he recalled the way that Merrill would listen and wait until just the right moment, when the emotional climate was ripe. Then, zing! Merrill delivered an eloquent interpretation that clicked right into place, just like the tongue and lock of a seatbelt, providing security and minimizing shock with his ever-so-confident, persuasive, smooth Anglo-accented air of authority. Merrill had a knack for penetrating straight into the heart of the matter, eventually arriving at the meaning of things that had once seemed hopelessly meaningless. Like a batter clearing the bases with a grand slam, crack! Merrill would bring it all home with his words. Carefully coached in his position by prominent psychoanalysts in London after the Second World War, he made interpretive plays with both ease and precision.

Ralph had felt secure in Merrill's hands, and that was no small thing. The sickening sights of brutality, butchery, and blood that Ralph was charged with examining at each horrific crime scene performed their reprise in his nightmares over too many months. The scent of iron, the torturous sensation of knives tearing through flesh and penetrating his own feelings; it was as if these atrocities were happening to him, until he'd wake up screaming. The result was suicidal ideation, which surfaced as his empathy toward and identification with the victims began to overcome his intellect and commonsense. He'd needed help, and he knew it. And it had worked. Ralph gradually began to trust his analyst with his soul. He learned to wait, not act. Although he sometimes hated to admit it, Ralph was certain that his own capacity for patience had increased during those three years on Merrill's couch. Patience had become a routine part of Ralph's day, an important feature of Ralph's character, of who he was.

* * *

After the door closed behind Rachael, Claudine sank back down into her chair. She remained in a state of reverie for some time, mulling over the feelings evoked in her heart and mind by that day's work. Her patients' unprocessed sensory experiences, all lined up like hungry little orphans seeking food for thought. Claudine took the time to bear the full effect of these unconsciously shared sensations for as long as it took to contemplate and to adequately understand them. If successful, this process would enable Claudine to gradually return these previously unprocessed happenings to her patients in a thoroughly detoxified, digestible and timely interpretation, accompanied by a benign attitude. She had that way of touching her patients with words, especially before and also immediately after their return from the break. Today, this crucial process left Claudine barely able to move, exhausted. Moments passed until she could even catch her breath.

Finally inhaling deeply, she regained some of her buoyancy. She removed her handbag from the drawer in her desk, found her compact and lipstick, and felt slightly more human again. Soon she'd be far away, even though the pain always lingered nearby. As she was tossed back and forth on waves of thought, it occurred to Claudine that the dolphin-baby in Rachael's dream bore a striking resemblance to another at-risk infant. Marta Orenstein had been born in pre-World War II Rumania. The pro-Nazi regime was just about to take over the country, soon to cooperate fully with Hitler's tyranny by deporting all Jews to the East. The rumors were of dark and dense camps, filled with Jews, gypsies, and homosexuals, abducted and enslaved, beaten and starved, and finally murdered.

All efforts were dedicated to the final solution of the Jewish problem. Their awareness of these realities terrified Marta's parents. Leo and Bess Orenstein were among those few who could face their inevitable fate. Fearing the worst, hoping for salvation, and grappling with the need to act, the couple fled with their baby daughter to Paris. As a poet and professor of some note who, like many of the Rumanian intelligentsia, had been heavily influenced by the French, Leo had gratefully accepted a timely invitation to take refuge in the French community, to teach and to write at the Sorbonne in Paris under the sponsorship of a wealthy expatriate who had dedicated his fortunes to rescuing as many of his Jewish brethren as possible.

In the beginning of 1939, it was a widely held belief, or at least a slim hope, that Hitler's march might be halted short of Paris by the potency of the vaunted Maginot Line. However, not long after arriving in Paris, Leo encountered an undeniable reality. The Nazis were huddled on the German border and entered France through Belgium in the Spring of 1940, ready to make their move, conquering the City of Light in less than two weeks. On the eve of that invasion, Leo and Bess placed little Marta in the home of a gallant and generous gentile family who was childless and lived across the hall. The Orensteins signed over the deed of their home to these neighbors, the Girards. They were uncertain that they would ever return to Paris and well-aware that Jewish property would most likely be confiscated by the Nazis.

The Girards welcomed their 'new daughter' with arms warm and wide. A delicate gold crucifix on a diminutive chain was immediately hung around Marta's chubby little neck, an amulet against the evil spirit of the Nazi invaders. Marta wailed as her parents released her reluctantly into the hands of these two virtual strangers. Leo kissed his wife and child goodbye one last time before disappearing in the company of two members of the French Underground who'd come to fetch him. With these two by his side and the cause before him, he might even have appeared more bold than heartbroken, looking through rather than at people they passed, jaw set, and brows furrowed.

Bess could barely remain upright, but she struggled to linger one more moment to place a final kiss on her baby daughter's moist and reddened cheek and she closed the door behind her, her own tears spilling down her pallid face. A stately blue-eyed blond and a skilled linguist originally of Germanic decent, Bess was easily able to create her own camouflage. With some expertly forged documents, Bess presented herself as one of those French citizens attached to the diplomatic corps and was quickly earmarked for service as a translator and interpreter for the occupying forces.

Before parting, Leo and Bess had agreed that if one or the other of them managed to survive the war, they'd attempt to retrieve their daughter from the Girards, and would do their best to gain passage on a ship to the United States. Leo's second cousin, Moishe, in New York, had provided contact information for each of them to memorize. Without much in the way of financial means and a blurry destiny ahead, their plan was neither well-conceived nor coordinated. Given the lack of time, all was sketchy at best. The pain that each had carried away in their rucksacks weighed them down like lead. Perhaps they never really believed that survival was possible, except through the existence and in the memory of little Marta.

CHAPTER 3

Remembering and Waiting

The case of the Sorrentino killings had threatened Ralph's psychic survival like no other, driving him into a deeply depressive anxiety that prompted him to seek analytic therapy with Merrill that first time around. The recurrent nightmares that preceded and followed the resolution of that investigation had kept Ralph in analysis for a few years. Now, he wasn't at all sure what had brought about the ending of his work with the good doctor. This time around another ending, a single unexpected death had brought him back for a second round of analysis. Surely Merrill wouldn't make him wait, lingering in his pit of grief. It had been exactly three months since Ralph's wife Dorothy had passed.

A long wait had begun for Ralph as Dorothy approached the end of a very different sort of wait. Ever since they'd first met and had fallen in love, Ralph and Dorothy dreamed of traveling the world together. But with four growing children, and Ralph's demanding work, there had never really been a good time for extended journeys abroad. Such foreign adventures would have to wait until the children were grown and Ralph had retired. They'd originally hoped for Ralph to leave the department at around age sixty.

At fifty-nine, things seemed to be on track. Still vigorous, Ralph was trim and tan. his wavy, salt and pepper hair had just begun to thin a little on top. But not so much that a man his age could complain. His cleft chin and nearly turquoise-blue eyes bore a likeness to Kirk Douglas, one of his favorite actors. These features, plus a neatly trimmed mustache, were set-off by a sun-kissed complexion and, except for a small scar that ran diagonally across his left cheek, he felt quite attractive.

Each day, rain or shine, he'd ridden his bicycle the three and a half miles from their home on the edge of Brentwood to the Beverly Hills Police Station. Dancing and biking were his-and-hers favorites on his days off. Ralph and Dorothy were passionate about each other, about family, and about life. She was an amateur photographer and loved to garden, and he had a go at stone sculpture. Their four children had given them six grandchildren, so far.

Dorothy appeared to be as vivacious as ever, enthusiastically involved with the children and grandchildren, growing flowers and vegetables, and creating dishes of a variety of cuisines. But one day—it was just three weeks before Ralph's sixtieth birthday—after their eldest daughter, Karen, had given birth to Lisa-Anne, their sixth grandchild, Dorothy was helping-out with the cooking and cleaning, and was playing with granddaughter Laurel when she suddenly keeled over on the lawn. Dorothy remained in a coma for months after her stroke.

Ralph waited, watched, even prayed over her faithfully. She never regained consciousness.

Time.

Ralph glanced at his wristwatch.

Late.

Merrill had never been late before. Maybe a sign of age. Ralph drummed his fingers on the table stacked with magazines next to the familiar cane bench on which he sat squirming. It was unlike Merrill to keep anyone waiting. *Maybe he's forgotten. No, not likely.*

He has a memory like a mentalist. There was never a time in those years with Merrill that Ralph had felt forgotten. Never did he feel that one detail of his life nor any moment of his time with Merrill had ever been confused, displaced, or lost.

It had always felt to Ralph that Merrill's capacity for memory was contagious, that he may have inherited Merrill's talent for reminiscing with complete accuracy and without fear of reprisal. In the sanctuary that was Merrill's disciplined mind, Ralph had been able to sort himself out from the victims and perpetrators that he had always been required to identify with in order to excel in his specialty. But loss was not a topic that had frequently made its appearance during that first piece of analysis, at least not personal loss experienced in a life filled with achievement, attainment, contentment, culmination, friendship, fruition, gratification, growth, hope, joy, romance and familial love.

Ralph had appeared fully confident, gratified and self-aware for several years as a result of his previous work with Merrill, until that recent, unexpected and premature loss of his darling Dorothy.

* * *

Marta was raised in the shelter of her new French Catholic family, the couple Francois and Michelle Girard. She felt loved and safe, even as Paris was at risk of being torn to pieces, exploded bridge by bridge, monument by monument. She grew to become a happy child. But when the war came to an end, Bess suddenly appeared one day to reclaim her daughter. As if she were some precious porcelain doll who had been left behind for safe-keeping, Marta was abruptly scooped up by a mother who'd been lost and long ago forgotten by the child for her own welfare and that of her caretakers. Bess had given little thought to what a child might feel for the mother and father who had protected and raised her from infancy, parents from whom she was now being torn away. Francois and Michelle tried to cajole Bess, reminding her that her apartment was still across the hall, kept in perfect order throughout the war years, the classical wooden furnishings still gleaming, the carpets and floors spared any speck of dust. But Bess was eager to travel to New York, to be reunited with Marta's father and her beloved husband.

However, it would prove even more difficult than anyone could have thought. Leo's cousin had died suddenly of a heart attack before the end of the war and had left no word for any of them. Leo seemed to have simply disappeared. Melancholy and loss became omnipresent for this mother and daughter, who barely knew each other. Each suffered from hurt and despair that they were unable to share, each aching with a sorrow for which there was no consolation, at least, none that existed in their rapport, which was thin and largely alienated.

Bess remembered Marta well, but her adoration for her child soon dissipated. For the little girl, Bess was a total stranger who had dragged her off to a foreign land. For this reason, Marta was unable to grant Bess even one word of encouragement, not even a hug or a kiss. By the time Marta realized that this strange, affectionate woman was indeed her biological mother, Bess had turned completely away from her daughter to protect herself from an unbearable disappointment that she could no longer tolerate.

One day, Marta and Bess received word that, after fighting quite bravely, Leo had been captured by the Nazis and had been held briefly for interrogation, until managing to escape to Switzerland. After the war, Leo immigrated from Geneva to the United States. With his cousin deceased, there was no word of Bess and Marta, and no means of contact. Fortunately, Leo was taken under the patronage of wealthy colleagues in the Department of Romanic Languages and Literature at the University of California at Berkeley. He flew directly to California, and in that sunny state in the late Fifties, the three refugees were reunited at last with the investigative assistance of The Hebrew Immigrant Aide Society.

A child with a complex history, Marta had been mercifully allowed to keep and to continue to grow up with the French name she'd been given. She continued, even under the care of Bess and Leo, to be known as Claudine Girard. The child's birth parents, irrevocably changed by the events of the war, must have sensed that it would only add to their little girl's sense of dislocation to saddle her with the now-unfamiliar name "Marta." But nothing could alter the fact that she had, in psychic reality, lost two mothers and two fathers in the war, all by the tender age of seven. Only as an adult, after she had begun working with patients, did Claudine fully suffer the loss of the baby-Marta that had once been herself. After coming to terms with her past, she became ideally suited for her chosen profession. With the assistance of her own analysis, she became a healer of lost, confused, and broken children whose distress often resonated with her own on one emotional plane or another. She had learned from experience that memories, as painful as they can be at first, are essential to the process of mending and restoring broken relationships, especially one's relationship with oneself.

The eventual resonance of feeling between Claudine and her own patients created a necessary (if not sufficient) foundation for a special bond between analyst and patient. This peculiar affiliation between two relative strangers made for a connection so compelling, it had the power to repair the most damaged of spirits, even when the roots of destruction were both elusive and subtle. For example, unlike Claudine, Rachael had not been overtly traumatized as a child. In fact, she was the beloved daughter of truly enlightened and loving parents. However, almost immediately after Rachael's birth, her mother became both emotionally and physically pre-occupied, not with her perfect newborn baby-girl, but with her three-year-old's fight for his life against acute lymphoblastic leukemia. The loss of her mother's undivided attention in that immediate post-partum period left Rachael with a sense of being unloved, unwanted, and forsaken. And now, in analysis, Rachael once again experienced that excruciating sense of being ripped off, of being denied a mother's steadfast attention, this time due to the five-week summer break in the analysis.

Claudine sat at her writing table, passing the time filling out insurance forms and composing instructions for the cleaning crew and the landlord. She always felt the need to tidy up loose ends before closing the office to go abroad. In a large carton, she'd begun to gather the potted plants together to bring home so that her housekeeper might tend them over the next month. She could hear the door to Alfred's consulting room open and close, the soft tread of footfalls on the interior hall carpet, followed immediately by the familiar click of the outer door of the exit hall, a sound that punctuated the end of Alfred's day.

The hands of the clock pointed to six. Alfred would step in to greet her soon enough. But in which state of mind? Merrill was a true Doctor Jekyll and Mr. Hyde.

Years earlier, at the end of one day, Jekyll appeared at the elevator where Claudine stood waiting. A twinkle in his eye, he held the door for her to enter. She barely knew him then; in fact, she only knew *of* him. Doctor Alfred Merrill was a famous psychoanalyst, formerly of London's Harley Street. Every analyst in Los Angeles, and in the rest of the country for that matter, had read a least some of his groundbreaking meta-psychological treatises—or, if not those, certainly his seminal papers that modernized therapeutic techniques with narcissistic patients.

Claudine stepped inside the elevator. Although she was a married woman, she felt like a swooning teenage girl in the presence of a matinee idol. She was flattered as he spoke to her throughout the four-floor descent to the lobby.

"Has your hair always been that elegant color?"

Claudine kept her eyes glued to the floor.

"Well, yes, since I was sixteen," she said.

She wondered what had caused him to suddenly notice her. They'd shared the elevator on and off for months since she'd begun working at the Roxbury Drive building. Until that moment, he'd never uttered so much as a good day.

"I suppose it's that lovely dress. It's the same silvery, silky hue, very much like your hair, so unusual on a young woman."

Merrill nearly crooned each word. Claudine dared to raise her eyes as he leaned back against the elevator wall, holding his attaché case at his groin with both hands. At first, he gazed into her eyes, then once more up at the ceiling.

"I once knew a young woman with silver hair when I was myself quite young." He added, "I fell in love with her at once."

He drifted off for a moment, lost in some sublime memory, as Claudine noticed his luminous blue eyes, set far apart below an unusually high if deeply furrowed brow. A split second later, he shook his head, as if blinking away his daydream. "But that was a very long time ago," he mused. "And I was so very, very young."

The remark seemed to signal Merrill's return to earth, just as the elevator came to rest on the ground floor. When the door slid open, sounds of traffic drifted in from the street, contaminating the nostalgic hush that embraced both of them. Merrill gestured with a mannered bow for Claudine to exit ahead of him. Stepping out into the lobby, Claudine felt her knees buckle just a bit. Her breath floated in her chest as if she had just landed from some celestial excursion without sufficient time to reacclimate to the weight of Earth's atmosphere.

And then there was Mr. Hyde. A ruthless sort, 'Hyde' spared no harsh words in the process of tearing down a young student in preparation for re-building him or her in his own ideological image—provided, of course, that the student presented as a willing subject for psychic renovation. Claudine had borne witness to the results of these didactic indoctrinations that masqueraded as therapeutic encounters. Of course, these 'training' analyses, as they were officially referred to, nearly always led to early career successes and financial security, although less fortunately they were coupled with a subtle impoverishment of authenticity, creativity, and genuinely innovative thinking. In short, Alfred castrated his young.

This was only half the reason that Claudine hadn't sought training with him. Of course, she'd suspected early on that the other half had something to do with her own strongly anachronistic attraction to this paternal figure with a passion for young gray-haired women, and the taboo against its realization.

Somewhat amused, Claudine now recalled how, over the years, these ambivalent feelings about Alfred Merrill had sorted themselves out in her heart and mind, finally allowing her to settle into a mental state balanced somewhere between realistic respect and admiration for Alfred's finer qualities, and a good-enough acceptance of her own feelings of disappointment with and about him and his more sinister doppelganger.

CHAPTER 4

Impatience and Intrusion

Anxious to leave for home to finish packing for her flight, Claudine gave in to a growing impatience with Alfred. She made her decision to close their waiting room. If he hadn't made an appearance after that, she'd have to roust him out. She walked into the hallway outside her consulting room and paused to straighten one of the framed posters on the wall, part of the Freudianna she and her husband, Bernard, had collected on their first visit to Bergasse 19 in Vienna and the Freud Museum in London.

From the beginning, when she was about to move into Merrill's suite, he'd encouraged her to decorate the hallway walls in any manner she wished—another of Merrill's *Jekyllian* gestures. Claudine had always loved this one poster. It showed an elderly Freud standing on the balcony of his Hampstead home in London with his two Chow dogs during the last year of his life. Deep in thought, Claudine was reminded of Bernard's affection for those big, furry, red, lion-like hounds, and how he'd longed to have one of his own. She felt a twinge as she flashed back on yet another image, a younger version of herself, who had put Bernard off the subject of adopting a dog more than a few times during their marriage. They both worked long hours and she believed that leaving a puppy alone all day was inhumane. She wondered now if this sense of the intrusion or abandonment that their work could impose on a puppy had been the product of her own projection.

"Just be patient, *Cheri*. As soon as we retire to our house in the country, I promise we will get a puppy, or even two."

She steadied her focus on the present, and tears welled up in her eyes as she re-experienced the pain and heartache of losing Bernard long before she could fulfill that promise and so many others. Turning away from the past, she opened the waiting room door.

"It's about time."

The man in the waiting room had snapped in jest, without so much as lifting his eyes from the *New Yorker*. When he finally did glance up, he looked startled.

"Oh, excuse me. I thought you were. . ." Ralph rose as he began his explanation.

Claudine interrupted. "Please, pardon my intrusion. You must be waiting for Doctor Merrill."

Claudine was stunned to find anyone seated in the waiting room at that hour. She thought it a strange time to schedule a consultation with a patient, if that was who this man was. She tried to identify her feelings. Annoyed? Perturbed? Suspicious? Unsettled was more accurate. Not that there was anything alarming about the way this man looked. He wore well-tailored gray flannel trousers, a starched white shirt, sleeves rolled up at the cuffs, and a red, black, and gray abstract tie, loosened beneath his unbuttoned collar. A gray silk herringbone tweed jacket lay folded on the bench beside him. It was already getting too warm in the room with the air conditioning turned off.

There was nothing threatening or even remarkable here. Or was there?

What stood out for Claudine were the various items attached to the man's black leather belt: A large ring with at least two dozen keys was fastened to his right side, and what looked like a large black, plastic walkie-talkie or an over-sized cell phone was clasped to his belt on the left. She suspected some sort of pistol sheathed in a lizard-skin shoulder holster. Next to that, something flickered and flashed. Something golden.

A badge?

A policeman. Perhaps he wasn't a patient after all.

"Is the Doctor expecting you?" Claudine asked, not waiting for the answer. "I'm certain he'll be with you soon."

As she backed up and shut the door, she hoped she hadn't been too intrusive. She was embarrassed by her own voyeurism, her impatience. Behind the door Claudine asked herself a question. Could he, if indeed he were a patient, be mistaken about the time? Or could Alfred have possibly *forgotten* a patient? Even Alfred could make an error. After all, he was human, sometimes.

She decided that it was time to knock on Alfred's door. Let *him* handle the stranger in the waiting room. But there was no reply. Maybe, she decided, he was deep in thought, or on the telephone. Pressing her ear to the wood only yielded the sounds of silence. If he was gone, why hadn't he left the door ajar? Claudine hesitated, then tapped again at the door. After a minute, she knocked louder. But she heard nothing but the hum of the ventilation system. She cracked open the door, barely peeking inside. The blinds sheers were closed, drapes drawn.

Peering through the darkness, she glanced first toward Merrill's desk. She saw stacks of journals and papers, bare silhouettes in a shadowy scene. Squinting, her eyes adjusted to the gloom as she entered. The murky shape of an open briefcase lay in one corner of the room. *He's still here.* A splinter of light escaped the curtained window, revealing an empty armchair. Turning her head slowly, Claudine caught sight of another shape, this one stretched out on the couch.

More detail came into focus as Claudine stared and blinked, frozen. It was Alfred. He looked tranquil, almost asleep; his face was relaxed. This, in itself, wasn't odd. He often took naps on his couch. But this time, there was something peculiar about the way he looked. And a strange odor pervaded the room. Claudine shivered as she made her way, one step at a time, toward the couch. In the dim light of his heavily draped chamber, the pool of blood in which Alfred reposed gradually distinguished itself from the sheen of his deeply tufted, burgundy leather divan.

* * *

Only a minute or two had passed since the attractive woman—who could only be Merrill's partner—had made her appearance, apologetically and rapidly retreating behind the waiting room door. Until that moment, Ralph Orloff had wondered what she was like. Curious about Claudine Ingersoll, PhD, Ralph had been hoping to catch a glimpse of her. He was impressed. She was a woman of elegant bearing, perhaps in her mid to late fifties or early sixties, sheathed in pearl-gray silk from head to toe. Dangling from her willowy neck was a long chain laced through a pendent that resembled a piece of fine contemporary sculpture.

Classy. She was tall and slender. Her hair, swept up in a loose French twist, barely exposed her delicate ears, subtly adorned by two *objets d'art* loosely related to the piece that hung near to the level of her slender waist. A lock of hair, gently brushed to one side of her forehead, accented a pair of bright aquamarine eyes that he wouldn't have minded staring into for several hours.

Perception or projection? Who knows? No matter. Ralph was tickled, if a bit guilty at the realization that he could have such imaginings about a woman so soon. Surely Dorothy wouldn't mind. It was the first time since her death that he'd even had a fleeting thought about another woman. Was he betraying her memory? Or was he thawing out?

Enjoy, he ordered himself. What's the harm? Couldn't hurt, could it?

Then a scream came from the interior of the suite.

Ralph seized his weapon. All reflexes, he rushed through the unlocked door from the waiting room, down the inner hall, and into Merrill's darkened office. He came to an abrupt halt at the sight of Doctor Ingersoll, hands covering her eyes, standing over Merrill's corpse, lying on the couch.

CHAPTER 5

Death is in the Details

The red brick facade of 450 Roxbury Drive was bathed in flashing lights of red, white, and blue strobes rotating atop three squad cars, each one angled into the curb from a different direction. They'd arrived at the scene in response to the call from Detective Orloff, reporting the homicide of one of couch canyon's most prominent tenants.

There had been few unnatural deaths of psychoanalysts in their own consulting rooms over the years. One had been a suicide by drugs and alcohol; one a murder by a patient's jealous husband; and one a fatal heart attack suffered in the course of a robbery. But none of these deaths had been quite as gruesome as the murder of Doctor Alfred Merrill.

Within minutes the team from the LA County Coroner's office rolled up, followed by the duty officers, and the usual compliment of investigators from CAPS, the four-detective detail assigned to handle all crimes against persons. Those present included Ralph's partner, Detective Benjamin Hollinger, Chief of Investigations Lt. Seth Rogers, the sergeant in charge of the CAPS detail, and none other than the big shot of the BHPD, Commissioner Forbes himself.

The media vultures soon began to circle outside the yellow crime-scene tape. Ralph knew they'd have a field day with this one. Merrill's patients would unfortunately hear the news of the murder without preparation, complete with graphic crime-scene photos. He could only hope that protocol would prevent this act of insensitivity. Advertisers and sponsors fed on this kind of sensationalism. Networks and newspapers cashed in as soon as they could by throwing chum to the sponsors. To add insult to injury, the pressure from City Hall was sure to be at maximum, with all the gory details coming out in the open on the late-night local breaking news and in the morning tabloids.

Upon entering the crime scene, the coroner came to a full stop, allowing time for the scene to speak to him. He listened carefully and articulated what the scene had said.

"The details are clear. The victim's throat was slashed nearly to the cervical bone, an act undoubtedly fueled by passion. Throughout, it appears the victim had been reclined on his leather couch in a three-piece suit, head resting on this pillow, legs extended, feet in a relaxed position. The victim appears to have been unconcerned by whatever led up to the attack. From all appearances, it seems that he'd been lying right here when he was attacked. His body wasn't moved."

Walking first one way, then another; picking up the victim's hands and dropping them gingerly, the coroner made additional conclusions.

"No overt signs of a struggle, nothing immediately perceptible under his well-manicured nails. It's possible he knew the murderer well enough to let him or her into the room. No sounds were reported. Preliminarily, we can deduce that the perp used an extremely sharp implement, possibly a surgical scalpel or a straight razor, about four inches long, finely honed, held in the left hand, blade turned like so."

The coroner's gesture indicated that the killer would have held the blade facing him or herself, drawing it across the victim's throat, then stepping away quickly. He beckoned for the gurney and body bag. "Looks like the blood is just about all here on the couch. You can see for yourself," he said, head bowed, navigating carefully around the path between the couch and the door, crouching down to get a better look at the pale ecru carpet.

"Time of death?" Ralph asked.

"I'd say roughly within two hours. Hmm, no footprints on the rug, not a drop on the floor. Not in the hall or outside the suite anywhere, for that matter, far as we can tell. The scan will confirm it, you can be certain about that."

Ralph felt queasy, an acid taste lingered on his palate and tongue. He was surprised at his own reactions. He'd seen worse over the years. But he'd never had so intense and specific a relationship with a victim before this. He shook his head as if to reset his thought processes, summoning his mind to settle his stomach.

"What about the elevator, the stairwell?"

"Checking now. They're going over it all with luminol and dusting. Polished brass and mirrors will yield evidence, if there's any in the elevator. That's including any attempt to hide it."

Ben addressed Rogers. "So, it's me and Ralph on this one, Chief?"

"Not sure," Rogers replied, shooting a glance at Ralph.

Ralph spoke immediately. "I want this one, Frank."

"I'll bet," Rogers said. His tone softened. "Look, Ralph, all you've got to do is say the word. You're out of here in just a few weeks. As far as this case is concerned, you're a witness to the scene. Besides, with Dorothy and all you've been through, maybe you need a break." Frank Rogers could see by Ralph's clenched jaw that his old friend was becoming even more obstinate than ever. Still, he kept trying. "I mean, don't you wanna go fishing or something, man? Bounce one of those little granddaughters of yours on your knee? Take a trip to the Bahamas?"

"The Bahamas will be there when this case is solved," Ralph said.

Rogers went on, even as he suspected it was futile. "Let it go to one of the young Turks, Ralph. You don't really need this fucking headache." He leaned in and said, in a confidential murmur, "The vic is a fancy B.H. shrink. Which means his patients have the mayor on speed-dial. You don't need the pressure."

Ralph leaned toward the Chief with his own confidential whisper. "I know, Frank. The vic was my shrink, too."

Roger's bushy eyebrows nearly brushed the ceiling. "No shit."

"Yeah. So—"

"Hang on." The Chief looked pensive. "We've got protocols about investigating the killing of your spouse or a close relative. We might have one about this."

Ralph smiled. "Pull the other one, it's got bells on it."

"I'm serious! I mean, it's not my thing, but a guy and his shrink—it's a special relationship, isn't it?"

Ralph nodded. "It is. But I doubt the Department's rules go that far. Besides, I hadn't seen Merrill in a while."

"Still—"

"Plus, you're short on manpower. The new guy won't get here until next month, Hong is tied up in the high school rape case, and the whole squad'll be sitting in the courtroom once the Menendez case goes to trial."

Rogers gave Ralph a deadpan stare. "Well, aren't you a dedicated public servant."

"I'm a saint. You know that." Ralph's tone shifted. "Besides, the woman who shared Merrill's suite . . . I didn't see a wedding ring. And believe me, I looked."

The Chief shrugged. "Okay. I tried. Maybe you should've practiced law with that degree of yours. You and Ben are on. I'll put in a request to extend your retirement date, at least until the case is closed."

Ralph stepped back as the morgue crew moved in with the gurney. It occurred to him that, not only did he find the idea of further contact with Merrill's colleague appealing, he could actually use her help on the case. Who was better placed to know the particulars of Merrill's practice, his patients, his possible conflicts with them and with those around them? Ralph hoped she wouldn't find the prospect of assisting a cop inappropriate or distasteful. Then again, it was a brutal killing, and he wouldn't blame her if she'd been shaken up and wanted nothing to do with it.

Hell, *he'd* been shaken up. That's why he'd been waiting in Merrill's office in the first place.

* * *

While men from the coroner's office and the crime lab continued to examine Merrill's office, Claudine retreated to the tiny, windowless galley that was little more than an oversized closet, just off the exit hallway. She prepared fresh coffee, poured herself a cup, and sat, watchful and waiting, within sight but out of the way at a small wrought iron café table set back in the corner of the cubicle kitchen.

Claudine found herself concentrating her gaze on the door of Alfred's room, still waiting for him to emerge, straight and tall in spite of it all. Her habitual deference to him as a senior colleague still prevailed. He'd earned it. He had mentored Claudine through the Institute training, discussing her debut paper at a meeting of the entire Society, even though she was an unknown and not a true believer in his particular brand of analysis.

Claudine owed him. She had neither been analyzed nor formally supervised by him—nor, for that matter, by any of his close followers. On occasion, she had even dared to disagree with him publicly. Yet he had always stood by her. They'd shared the suite for some five years after she lost Bernard. Claudine's mood grew black. Tears streaming, her head faltered and collapsed against one arm stretched across the table. She saw the face of Bernard, the only man she'd ever been able to give herself to with recklessness. A young U.S.

Army pediatrician, stationed at Great Ormond Street Hospital in London after the second world war, he'd met Claudine when she was still a student in Geneva working with the famous Professor Piaget, and visiting London for a conference.

* * *

No messages. Ralph hung up the phone and walked into the kitchen. Claudine didn't move. Ralph stepped over to her and placed his hand on hers. She looked up into his face. He was relieved to see her smile come back to life.

"Hope you don't mind," he said. "I could really use some of that coffee right now."

" I made it for you—and your men, of course."

She patted the chair beside hers, a welcoming gesture for him to join her. On cue, Ralph poured a cup for himself and sat down.

"Do you need to call someone?" he asked. "Your family, your husband? It's getting pretty late."

He self-consciously looked at his watch. "Eight-thirty now."

"I was just thinking of him," Claudine mused aloud.

"Him?"

"Bernard, my husband. He died of cancer—years ago."

"I'm sorry."

"It was the same year that Alfred's colleague died. It pleased Alfred that I agreed to take his place here. There were many who had idealized and even idolized Alfred since he came to Los Angeles from London. There were also those colleagues who attacked him for his theoretical positions. But my husband and I were always objective where Alfred was concerned."

"So, he had enemies?"

"Enemies? Some, I suppose. Or perhaps you'd call them adversaries. Some people disagreed with the way Alfred ran the

Institute—although Bernard and I often felt that their objections had more to do with their clinical or theoretical predilections. But Alfred had many allies as well. Bernard and I rallied to his defense in political and educational matters, and Bernard gave him sound council over the years." She paused. "Is all this really relevant?"

Trying not to smile, Ralph said, "Anything you can tell me is relevant."

Claudine shrugged. "I think Alfred relied upon us for our candor, however much we disagreed with him theoretically. I think he trusted us much more than the so-called faithful. So, it was quite natural for me to move into this suite. I sublet the one I had shared with my husband, just two doors down and across the hall. Now I was just waiting to say goodbye to Alfred before our summer holiday. I was on my way to visit my father in Geneva."

"You're Swiss?"

"Rumanian, originally. Father moved into a country home outside Geneva after my mother passed away, nearly fifteen years ago. I will need to make some arrangements."

"Go right ahead," Ralph gestured to the doorway.

"I suppose my departure will need to be postponed. I'm certain you will be wanting a statement from me. Perhaps I could be of some help to you in the investigation as well. You will want someone to handle Alfred's patients, *non*?"

"He and his wife were flying abroad, too?"

"Yes. He to London, Lucienne to Paris. And what about yourself? You were here to see him, were you not?"

"Is it that obvious? Or are you psychic?"

She gave a slight smile. "You were in his waiting room. Or did you intuit that he would be murdered?"

He sat back and laughed. "I'm good, but I'm not that good. Yes, in fact I had been seeing him a while ago. I came back for a quick tune-up." He suddenly looked dubious. "If there is such a thing."

"Tune-ups, yes. Quick? Well . . ."

Both of them paused. It struck Ralph that she had every opportunity to leave. Yet she seemed quite comfortable and in no hurry. So he figured, what the hell. "As long as you're here . . . and you seem willing to postpone your trip . . . I wonder if I can ask for your assistance in this case. It would be unofficial, and of course feel free to say no. But you seem familiar with Doctor Merrill's background, and how this place functions . . . and, now that I think of it, you might be able to help me get inside the head of the perp."

She looked intrigued. "Detective—"

"By 'perp' I mean, the person who murdered him. The perpetrator."

She gave him a chiding look. "I know what 'perp' means. I do own a television. And it so happens I am a great fan of the *romans policiers*. That means—"

"I know what '*romans policiers*' means. Or I can guess. I know it doesn't mean some cops in Italy."

"*Voila.*"

There was a pause. Each stifled a smile. Ralph found himself hoping this conversation could go on for the next two years.

Finally Claudine said, "I will be happy to help you in any way I can. And we can be thankful for one thing. There won't be the day-to-day interference to contend with, since we were just closing the offices for a month."

"That *is* a break," Ralph said. "For his patients, too, I suppose."

He thought about how easy it was to lose sight, at least for the moment, of the fact that he was one of those patients. Did it matter? Chief Rogers had sort of feinted in that direction but then seemed to let it go. Just as the question threatened to get sticky, Ralph was rescued by Ben.

"Hey, Ralph." Ben barged in as though entering a locker room. He came up short when he saw Claudine. "Oh, 'scuse me. Umm, that coffee does smell good. May I?" He poured a cup without waiting for a response. "Mm, mm. Good stuff. I needed that. So, we're about to release the body to the coroner, just about wrapped up in there for now. The scene is secure. Walter's people are down the hall. I was about to take Officer Gordon with me to cover the floors. Not too many offices open, I suspect. Most don't have receptionists anyway, so there's hardly anyone to talk to tonight. May have to wait 'til the morning, maybe Monday."

"Probably," Ralph said. "Most of the tenants in the building are either analysts or some other kind of therapists, psychologists, psychiatrists—which means almost no one has a front office. If they're in, the waiting room doors will be unlocked. Why don't you go turn some doorknobs, flip some switches and push some buttons and see who's in, while I wind things up here. We'll touch base later?"

"Right. After I check out the building, I'll get back over to the station and start in on the paperwork. Later."

Ben waved, as he took a last gulp, put down the cup, tipped an invisible cap as a gesture of courtesy to the lady doctor, and wandered out of the room.

"I don't think I have ever seen anyone so un-self-conscious as that young man," Claudine said.

"Yeah," Ralph said. "He's the department's free spirit."

Ben Hollinger was the personification of laid-back. His twang and shuffle betrayed his deep Southern origins. His beige-blond hair, fair skin, and neat mustache, all packaged in a palomino-colored seersucker suit and creamy calf-skin cowboy boots, made him resemble a cop from a tv-buddy series. Although the lines in Ben's forehead attested to his forty years, he gave the impression of a carefree kid playing cops and robbers. Which was to say, not quite the look of a man investigating what was sure to be considered one of the most sensational crimes to hit that glamorous town in quite a while—at least the most sensational since the Menendez brothers shot-gunned their parents to death in their three-plus million-dollar mansion in the flats below the hills of Beverly.

"When was Doctor Merrill leaving for London?" Ralph asked.

"Tonight. We were all leaving tonight. Which reminds me, I really must call Lucienne. On second thought, that wouldn't be right. I can't break this news to her on the telephone. Detective, it's only a few blocks from here, and she will be worried to death, it is so late."

"Of course, you're right. I'll go with you. it may be important for me to witness Mrs. Merrill's reaction to the news of her husband's death."

Claudine hesitated, surprised. "Really?"

"At this point, everyone's a potential suspect."

She tried to speak, but suddenly—you could never predict what detail or comment would be the one to shatter someone's self-control—the tears started. Ralph pulled a fresh, neatly folded handkerchief from the back pocket of his slacks and handed it over to her.

"*C'est pas possible*," she gasped. "This horrible thing." She took the handkerchief with a weak smile of thanks and spent some seconds composing herself. She sighed. "But I suppose it must come home to roost now, the reality of his death. Someone has butchered him and we don't know who it is. This undermines any sense of safety. What I mean to say is, who can you trust when nearly everyone is under suspicion? *Mon Dieu*, I was right in the next room."

"Yes, you were," Ralph said. "And what about that? Did you hear anything? Or see anyone?"

"I don't know. Truly. I heard nothing. *Des murs maudits !*"

"Excuse me ?"

"These damned walls. They're soundproof. If they weren't, I might have heard something. Perhaps I could have prevented it and he'd still be alive." She gave a little laugh. There was no pleasure in it. "I feel responsible. Of course, I am not. But still."

Ralph reached into his coat pocket, pulling out a package of cigarettes. He tugged at the plastic, opened the pack, and tapped one out. Claudine, eyes wide, accepted it with a gesture that reminded

Ralph of ballet. As she stared into his eyes, he felt ignited. The muscles in his jaw quivered as he cupped his hands, bringing the match near to her forlorn face. She dragged deeply with eyes closed.

"I really would appreciate it if you would accompany me to see Lucienne," she said. "To tell her. Thank You, Detective . . .?"

"Ralph, Ralph Orloff."

"Ralph," Claudine said. "And I am Claudine Ingersoll." She extended a hand in mock formality.

"*Enchantée.*"

He shook it. "You and me both."

CHAPTER 6

The Final Hour and The First Meeting

Ralph and Claudine drove in silence through the moonlit flats, past imposing one and two-story Spanish haciendas, colonial mansions, and Italianate villas. Crossing Sunset Boulevard, Ralph jogged to the left toward the canyon. He wondered who had exited Merrill's office at six that evening. He'd heard the exit door's familiar *click-swish* that had always proclaimed the upcoming appearance of his analyst at the waiting room door.

Eager for him to appear, Ralph had arrived at Merrill's office by five fifty-five, although his appointment wasn't until six-ten. He flipped open the latest copy of *The New Yorker*. Unable to concentrate, he let his eyes wander from the magazine to the hunt prints hanging about the walls of the six-by-eight compartment that was Merrill's waiting room. He took inventory of the few items of furniture, the small cane-back bench, two modest Victorian chairs, and a curio lamp table topped with magazines. Nothing had changed since his last visit.

He began to recall that final hour with Doctor Merrill.

It had been nearly fifteen years ago. In fact, that appointment was, like today's, Merrill's last opening before the summer holiday break. Ralph recalled the dream he'd had the night prior to that final session, a dream that captured the entirety of that terminal hour as well as the meaning of the analysis, from its beginning to its end. The image was still crystal clear, as if he were only just now awakening from the dream.

He was driving down Little Santa Monica in the left lane and someone in a silver Mercedes behind him was leaning on his horn, wanting him to pass the car holding up traffic in front of him. Ralph couldn't discern what was ahead because it was dark and somehow, he had shrunk so that, like a little boy, he could barely see over the steering wheel. The driver behind him kept honking the horn and nearly got them both killed as he passed him, speeding like a bat out of hell.

Ralph kept driving until he reached home. He pulled his car into the driveway in front of his house. He could see that someone had preceded him into the driveway, overshooting the pavement and crashing straight through the picket fence, causing considerable damage to the front entrance of the house and the garage door.

Ralph looked at the point where the vehicle had hit the fence and found flecks of silver paint, which appeared to have come from the vehicle. He was pissed off, certain that the motherfucker who had rammed his fence and hit the entrance and garage was the same sonofabitch that had just passed him on the road. He barged through the front door, only to discover that the driver who had damaged the outside of his house had also gotten inside.

What a mess.

People were partying all through the house.

Ralph didn't recognize a single soul. He supposed that all the intruders had been invited in by this careless stranger with the silver 450SL. The inconsiderate lout had apparently fled the scene, leaving all kinds of strangers inside, eating and drinking, bullshitting and just generally lousing the place up and, to add insult to injury, ignoring Ralph when he came through the door.

Some blond brought out two sumptuous trays of food from the kitchen, but she passed him by as if he were invisible. She made him feel ravenous. He snarled as he went from room to room, gradually realizing that these 'party animals' were really just a bunch of old ladies. They were hanging out in every room of his house, lounging on every chair, couch and table, occupying every surface.

Ralph had a tough time trying to figure out how to handle the situation, when he suddenly noticed that one of them was using his police radio and another was messing with his .38 caliber revolver. That did it! Before he lost his cool altogether, he had to take control.

He called the old women to order with a gavel, banging on the table like a superior court judge. As he did, he was relieved to find out that he had not only regained his former stature but that he could handle these old biddies without tossing them out of the house and doing them bodily harm.

Ralph had awakened from the dream feeling satisfied with himself. He couldn't wait to get his hands on that hit-and-run driver in the silver Mercedes. On the couch that last day, he let his mind wander, associating freely to each of the elements of the dream, knowing there was no time to waste in that final hour.

Merrill drove a silver Mercedes. He was the 'driver behind,' just as he sat behind Ralph while Ralph had reclined on the couch all those years. Merrill was the driving force behind the analysis.

"You're feeling pushed by me to terminate our contact," Merrill told him. "And you're terrified when you feel very small and unable to see what's ahead. This may reflect a diminished sense of your own omnipotence since the beginning of the analysis. Now you are in touch with that fearful little-boy aspect of yourself, aware of your own vulnerability seated firmly in a realistic sense of your own mortality, a reality you have largely evaded since childhood. You seem on some level to experience the end of your analysis as being overtaken and surpassed by me, another feeling you had denied as a child and ever since your own Father's death."

Merrill had been right. Ralph's father had died of tuberculosis when the boy was only eight years old. Consequently, Ralph had always harbored the fantasy that he'd won the favor of his mother by defeating a weakened rival.

"You entered adolescence prematurely," Merrill had continued. "With both an illusion of immortality and an exaggerated sense of complete and total responsibility for your mother's welfare. It's no wonder that your emotional armor began to deteriorate when you were faced with the Sorrentino serial killings."

Ralph's attention was jolted to the present when Claudine said,

"We shall be turning off to the left, just up here a bit." She indicated a long, tree-shaded driveway. Ralph suddenly realized that he would actually see his analyst's home. It was hard to grasp.

Sixty yards or so ahead, the asphalt lane opened out into a clearing in front of a sprawling ranch-style house. Set at the back of the oversized flag lot, the Merrill home was hidden from the main road. It was a perfectly private hideaway, complete with stables, a small riding arena, and a guest house, which was lit up and appeared to be occupied.

As Ralph parked the car, he blanched. It was as if he were violating Merrill's privacy. They were approached by a good-looking man in his early thirties. Clad in jeans, a plaid flannel shirt, and worn but polished riding boots, the man emerged from the tiny cottage, alerted by the sound of tires on the gravel and the warning neighs of the stable's occupants.

"Hiya, Doc," he said in a Western drawl. "I would 'a thought you'd be on your way to the airport by now. Boss's not back yet, but Lucy's in the stable. Actually 'spected you were him. She's fit to be tied. Maybe you can settle 'er down some." Turning to Ralph with his hand outstretched, the cowboy addressed him.

"Name's Kurt, Kurt Cross."

"Ralph Orloff," the detective replied, shaking the coarsened mitt.

"Too bad you two didn't get here a mite sooner. You just missed the show. Fancy, she's the Missus' favorite mare, was out with her new colt in the arena 'til a minute or two ago. That little stud can sure flex his hocks, and let there be no doubt, he's gonna be quite a stud. His mamma doesn't look too bad herself on these cool evenings. So, what can I do fer yah?"

"Nothing at the moment, Kurt," Claudine said. "We will just show ourselves out to the stable, if that's alright."

"Suite yourself, Ma'am. Guess I'll just get on with loading up the luggage into the Mercedes. Nice meeting yah, Mister Orluv, sir."

Kurt turned and ambled off, leaving Claudine and Ralph to find their way to the four-stall barn.

"Kurt's their hired hand?"

"So to speak, although he's really much more than that to them. He does everything from the gardening, to caring for the horses, to the grocery shopping. Sometimes he even cooks. He's been like a son to Alfred and Lucienne. You see, Kurt was orphaned as a young adolescent, a child from the Camden Center. One of the less disturbed ones, but still from an abusive home."

Ralph nodded. "I know the place. Those kids who end up there have had it tough. The fella that runs it used to be an analyst himself, wasn't he?"

"Yes, Don Dickens. Kurt had it worse than most, though. His family was originally from Texas. His father couldn't hold down a job when they moved to LA. And the wife had no skills. Kurt's father drank and simmered and ranted until one night he killed his wife in an alcoholic rage. He'd taken a knife from her hand as she was preparing dinner. Perhaps it was remorse that drove him off the edge of Topanga Canyon Road that same night."

Small world, Ralph thought. He had been involved in another case at the time. Anthony Sorrentino had butchered several women earlier that spring, around Mother's Day 1970. A half-dozen bodies had been discovered by the time the police could get their act together. There hadn't been such a series of brutal killings in the city's history in years.

Besides the modus operandi, all the victims had one thing in common. Each had had a son. The women ranged from a well-to-do elderly lady who owned a penthouse condo on Burton Way, to a twenty-seven-year-old waitress who rented an apartment off Olympic Boulevard and Doheny Drive.

Each woman had been discovered bound to her bed with silk scarves, raped repeatedly, this only after their breasts had been carved off their chests, the knife running along the backbones and under the arms as if they were Thanksgiving turkeys. As a finishing touch, Sorrentino had cut out their hearts, attaching a note to each that simply read *Happy Mother's Day!*

Before Orloff and his then-partner, Max Rydell, had solved the mystery and apprehended the killer, Sorrentino had ended the lives of seven more mothers, leaving more than a dozen orphaned sons to mourn their mothers' hideous deaths.

In Ralph's deepest unconscious fantasy, Anthony Sorrentino *was* his enraged Father, returned from the grave to assert his right to possess Ralph's mother, taking revenge on both by savagely murdering her and leaving Ralph to mourn repeatedly in identification with all those now-motherless sons, the indirect victims of Sorrentino. Ralph had been nearly overwhelmed by the helplessness he'd experienced during the many months of that investigation. He'd almost lost his own life during Sorrentino's capture. The night terrors were the last straw that sent him collapsing onto Merrill's couch.

His thought rambled off again to his termination dream, the 'souls' Ralph couldn't recognize. Those who had taken up residence in his house were clearly the ghosts representative of all those murdered mothers. And how different, fundamentally, were Sorrentino's homicidal impulses, and Ralph's own murderous feelings, feelings that had occupied every chamber of his mental life? The "dead" women of his dream represented aspects of his own mother, a woman who had completely occupied him since he was a fatherless boy, demanding his full attention, his heart and soul, until she finally died of breast cancer when Ralph was at the University.

In the dream, the *superior* court judge, who was finally able to take control of these rowdy, intrusive, and demanding mothers, stood for that part of Ralph that had been, and still was to this day, possessed by an overly strict sense of duty toward his work, and an almost religious devotion to the law.

Ralph realized that not having to evict the *old biddies* from his home in the dream meant that he was now more able to bear those previously intolerable aspects of his relationship with his mother. He had thought that not having to do them bodily harm meant that he had been relieved of the extremes of guilt that he'd borne as a mother-killer in his unconscious—the only place that he could allow the excesses of his resentment toward his own mother to cross his mind.

On yet another level, it seemed hopeful that in the dream he'd also experienced his anger toward the father for surpassing him. That is, for partying with mother before his arrival—preceding his birth—and for leaving him with *the mess* to deal with after Father's departure due to his pre-mature death from tuberculosis. This, at the time, might have been sparked by the possibility that Ralph had felt that Merrill, too, was leaving him with an internal mess to handle all on his own on that terminal day.

And it was possibly also true now, once again, with his death.

In the final analysis, Ralph began to feel that he was up to the task of carrying on the mental and emotional work of a self-analysis without further assistance from Merrill.

But was he really ready, or was it just a dream?

Ralph's attention returned once again to the conversation with Claudine.

"I remember the case of Kurt's father," he said. "About a dozen years ago, wasn't it?"

"Yes. After a short time, Jillian De Mayo, Kurt's therapist at the Center, asked Alfred if he knew anyone who might consider fostering such a child. Jill was in supervision with Alfred at the time. She knew he owned horses and Kurt was fond of animals. She tried to make a match."

"Wise woman."

"Wise and well-meaning. One thing led to another and Lucienne and Alfred took Kurt into their home for what was to be an interim period. But, as you can see, he has never left them. They even adopted Fred just for Kurt."

"Fred?"

"Kurt's Jack Russell terrier."

They arrived at the entrance to the barn. At that moment, as if his name were a call to action, out of the barn darted a small brown and white dog, leaping straight into Ralph's arms. Ralph smiled.

"Friendly little fellow."

Lucienne Merrill stood in the aisle of the barn, gazing into one of the stalls. She was an elegant woman, with raven-black shoulder-length hair cut in a stylish wedge that framed a face blessed with glistening olive skin and colossal almond-shaped, jade-green eyes. She was decked out in red suede jodhpurs tucked neatly into knee-high black boots, and a black, cowl-neck cashmere sweater that revealed a youthful cleavage, belieing her sixty-plus years.

As the two women approached each other and embraced, it seemed to Ralph that Lucienne was a perfect *Rose Red* to Claudine's *Snow White*.

"Claudine, *Cherie*, you look wonderful," the older woman said, bestowing her friend with air kisses. "What a surprise to see you. I should have thought you would be at the airport by now. It is almost getting too late for us. Alfred is always so thoughtless, but this? What is he thinking of?"

Turning to Ralph, eyeing him with curiosity, she beamed.

"*Allo Monsieur*. I do not think we have had the pleasure."

"This is Ralph Orloff, Lucienne," Claudine said, as Ralph offered his right hand.

"It is always a pleasure to meet a friend of Claudine's. I was just going to pour myself a glass of wine in the tack room. Would you two care to join me?"

Without waiting for the answer, she turned, walking away, a catty look on her face. "*Desolé*, I am usually a bit on edge before we go abroad and I am afraid tonight is no exception, especially with Alfred so late."

Lucienne glanced over her shoulder as she led the way to the end of the barn aisle, stopping at a door opening onto a pine-paneled room that resembled a small drawing room in an old-fashioned hunting lodge. Before entering, she suddenly spun around. A touch of concern darted across her eyes. "I hope Alfred has not encountered some crisis with a patient. I expected him long before now."

"Lucienne, I have something to tell you."

"*Zut alors*! Then he has sent you to soften me up about his tardiness?"

"Please, Lucienne. Come. Let's sit a moment inside where we can have that glass of wine."

Claudine placed her arm around the older woman's shoulder, guiding her through the passageway. She looked back at Ralph as if counting on him to block any move on her part to escape the difficult task she knew she must now carry out.

Inside the tack room, Lucienne took down three weighty, elegant Lalique leaded crystal wine glasses from a small cabinet above a refrigerator, out of which she withdrew what appeared to be a previously-opened bottle of Chardonnay. As she poured the wine, her graceful back turned toward her two unexpected guests as she spoke with an eerie hush. "Something has happened to Alfred, has it not? It is why you are here instead of on your way to Geneva, *n'est-ce pas*?

Claudine and Ralph remained silent.

"And your friend here," she said. She turned toward them where they sat on opposite ends of the leather sofa and held out two of the glasses, one in each of her shaky hands. She looked Ralph over with great interest as he accepted the glass. "I suspect he is not a friend at all, although it would do you much good if you were to have such an attractive friend, *Cherie*."

"You're right, Mrs. Merrill," Ralph said. "I'm afraid I'm not a friend of Doctor Ingersoll. I'm a detective," he said as he presented his badge. "Beverly Hills Police Department. Something has happened this evening." He rose to take the other wine glass from Lucienne's increasingly unsteady grasp.

As he spoke, Claudine got up from the sofa and walked over to Lucienne's side, helping her into an overstuffed chair, perching herself on its left arm. Placing one hand on Lucienne's right shoulder, Claudine leaned in to face her friend and uttered the words that Lucienne would never have anticipated. "Alfred is dead."

Lucienne made a fist, digging her bright red fingernails deep into her own palms.

"Alfred has been murdered, Lucienne."

"*Mon Dieu, non,*" Lucienne cried out, searching Claudine's face before burying her own in the bodice of her friend's dress. After a few moments she looked up, first at Claudine, then at Ralph. Tears splashed off her long eyelashes. "How? Who could have? Why? How did it . . .?"

"We don't know who or why anyone would want to harm Alfred. That is what Mr. Orloff is hoping to find out. And we can help him by answering his questions, my dearest."

"But how? Where? When? I have my own questions."

"It must have been between five and six this evening," Claudine said. "It was just before I took my five o'clock patient in from the waiting room that I saw Alfred in the kitchen, taking some aspirin," Claudine recalled.

Ralph pulled out a pen and a small notepad from his jacket pocket. Claudine briefly nodded toward him, as if in approval of his note taking.

"I may forget these things later, but at this moment it all seems too clear. May I go on? Later I heard someone leave Alfred's office. It must have been right at six. Alfred's last patient usually comes at five-ten. I did not think anything out of the ordinary had occurred when I heard the door to the outer hallway close. I was merely waiting for Alfred to come out. But he seemed to be taking so much time, so I decided to close up the reception area while I waited. When I found Detective Orloff in the waiting room, I went looking for Alfred to let him know that someone was waiting for him. That's when I found him. Oh Lucienne, his throat was cut" Claudine said, her words turning into sobs. "*Quell horreur!*"

This time, it was Lucienne who had found enough inner strength for both of them, as she wound her arms around Claudine's neck, pressing Claudine's head into Lucienne's thick black mane, her cries rocking them both for some long moments.

CHAPTER 7

Empathy and the Women

Ralph couldn't help but be affected by the suffering of the women seated before him. All the same, they were suspects. He had to interrogate Merrill's widow and, although she had already given her statement, he would have to keep a close eye on Ingersoll throughout the investigation. He couldn't let personal attraction affect his objectivity.

Leaving the two women at Merrill's home late that night, Ralph returned to the murder scene. With the team gone and the body removed, there was space for deliberation. Alfred's appointment book lay on one side of the ornate mahogany desk. Ralph paged through the journal. He noticed the entry at five-ten on that day. Handwritten in red ink, next to the name *Michael,* were the letters 'OT'. In the entry for six-ten was his own first name and last initial.

Ralph wondered if Ingersoll would be able to assist him in decoding the various notations he saw scattered in the margins beside other names in the agenda. He was glad that they had arranged to meet in the morning at headquarters, where Lucienne would make her official identification of the body in the city morgue. Claudine had offered to accompany her friend to the police station, and from there to drive back to the office with Ralph to help sort through the records of the deceased.

It was after midnight when Ralph decided to lock up the scene and go home for the night. But home was only an empty house filled with the nightmares he'd struggled with since Dorothy had first fallen into a coma. That dream had brought him back to Merrill. It was almost always the same.

He walks up the driveway to the front porch. Dorothy sits on a swing. She looks just the way she had when they first met, with deep auburn hair, pulled up on the sides and loose behind, falling in a dense wave down her back, almost to her waist. Her green eyes gleam at the sight of him, enchanting in her lucent complexion, which was adorned by a few well-placed freckles atop two rounded cheekbones set high on each side of her heart-shaped face.

Dorothy gets up and seductively begins to walk toward him, her graceful arms outstretched. But before they can reach one another, she disappears into a sinkhole, calling for him to rescue her, the echo of her voice slowly evaporating in air. Try as he might, she's so far down into the blackness that he can't see her, can't touch her. As he awakens, her faded voice is replaced by his own muted cries for help.

With Merrill dead, those cries would never be answered. Or so he feared. Certainly not by Merrill. Probably not by anyone else, at least not for the time being. Ralph was somewhat consoled by the knowledge that the sinkhole of his own depression could be temporarily sidestepped. He felt that surge of adrenalin-boosted vitality lifting him up and away from his own cavern of grief in response to both the call of duty and his desire for revenge.

Ralph was confident that he could track down his analyst's murderer. He decided to stay a while longer and wandered into Claudine's room. It struck him that finding another analyst might be a more difficult task than solving the case. Eyeing her couch, he noticed how unlike Merrill's it was—and how essentially feminine. A soft floral tapestry in muted Victorian shades of dusty rose, gray, and French blue, covered an antique frame supported by four honey-stained claw feet. However, like Merrill's couch, it didn't invite sitting upright. Like all analysts' couches, it lacked arms, a back, or cushions to lean against or to prop up with. It was too deep from front to back, too low to the floor for accommodating a seated position. A pillow lay at one end with a dental bib draped over it, plastic side down. Its mauve-colored absorbent quilting lay face-up, welcoming a head heavy with sorrow and tears. The matching square swatch of fabric pinned at the opposite end of the couch marked a spot for tired feet to rest, with or without shoes.

That first consultation, Ralph had entered Merrill's room with discomfort. Ahead of him, a commodious leather club chair squatted across from the odd-looking, tufted leather divan, which resembled an old-fashioned fainting couch. Ralph chose the chair at once. The doctor, a half-head taller than himself and clad in a three-piece black suit and a white French-cuffed shirt, followed Ralph into the room, locking the door behind himself. Merrill took his place in an imposing leather wingback chair positioned at the end of the couch, where a leather pillow covered by a common paper towel seemed to lay in wait.

During his first few encounters with Merrill, Ralph's eyes repeatedly drifted over to that curious piece of furniture. He was fascinated by the couch, drawn to it like a paperclip to a magnet. Before he knew it, curiosity had gotten the better of him. By the third hour of consultation, he found himself willingly lying flat on his back. It happened so quickly, that he could hardly remember what Merrill looked like. Max Von Sydow, he thought now. Or was it his own father's features he recalled?

The couch was like a magic carpet, aiding his escape from the constricting bonds of a certain kind of inhibition that often goes hand in hand with Jewish neuroticism—Or at least from the kind of self-consciousness that can be destructive to the process of imaginative introspection that analysis depends upon. Little did Ralph realize then that this freedom was as important for the analyst as it was for the patient, allowing a linking of unconscious to unconscious, a sort of *mind-meld* that transcended the confinements of external reality.

The mere state of not being able to see each other somehow facilitated the exploration of the internal world. They were each of them at liberty to roam the psyche, each other's and their own, and to see more clearly backward in time. This sense of freedom enabled the transfiguration of past history into present happenings, and with it a metamorphosis of childhood myth and misunderstanding into new perspectives, eventually fortified by a tolerance of self and other.

As he sat down in the center of Claudine's couch, Ralph slipped off his loafers. He stretched out with his feet up and his hands clasped behind his head and gazed around the room, gradually drifting off into a deep, dreamless slumber. At ten past six, the coppery odor of blood lingering in the air throughout the office suite awakened him. He felt more than a little bit ghoulish, having slept so peacefully amid the scent of Merrill's death. Sitting up and squeezing into his shoes, he walked over to the large French windows. Unfastening the latches, he threw them open to let the fresh summer morning's breeze flow over his sleep-moistened skin.

* * *

Kurt turned the Mercedes around in the driveway and waited. As he watched the two women in black walking, heads down, arm in arm out of the front door of main house, he jumped from the car, sprinting to the passenger side and opening both front and back doors at once.

"It's alright, Kurt, I can drive," Lucienne said, incensed that he would treat her with such formality. She pushed past him, walking around to the left side of the car even before he could launch a protest.

"But Ma'am, I was only. . ."

"Please, Kurt, I *am* alright. Do not treat me like a child. I refuse to cave to your attempt to replace Alfred before he is even in the ground."

"Lucy!" Claudine cried. "How can you be so crude?"

"Surely you are not going to treat me like a child as well?" Lucienne snapped back.

"I assure you, I have no intentions of treating you like a child, Lucienne. But I do think you are acting like one. You owe Kurt an apology. After all, he was only being considerate of you."

Coolly, Lucienne said, "Thank you, Kurt for all of your kindness and sympathy, but if you insist on going to this event—"

Claudine was incensed. "Lucienne, really—"

"—then you may be seated in the back. And as for you, my dear Claudine, you will sit here by me, and remind me of the way to the police station, *n'est-ce pas?*"

Compliantly arranged inside the car, Kurt and Claudine shut their doors.

Lucienne checked her lipstick in the rear-view mirror once more. Then she put the car in drive and sped down the driveway, turned into Beverly Drive, crossing Santa Monica Boulevard, and headed toward that peculiar mixture of old Spanish baroque and new art deco-style buildings that coalesce to make up the Beverly Hills Civic Center.

* * *

Ralph found a small powder room off the two analysts' kitchen. He splashed his face with cool water, dried off with paper towels, locked the suite behind himself, and left for home. Driving with the top down on his red '70 Buick Centurion convertible, and passing lawns glistening with dew at the crack of dawn, always made him feel younger—twenty-eight years younger, to be exact. But that wasn't the only reason he'd kept the Buick all these years. Ralph was never one to throw away something good in favor of something new.

On San Vicente, Ralph passed several early morning joggers and cyclers along the meridian of the upper middle-class community of Brentwood. On 26th Street, he cruised uphill and bore left around the curve by the junior high school, finally turning onto Allenford Street and into the driveway of the single-story house where he and Dorothy had raised their four children. They'd lived in this house for more than twenty-five years.

He still enjoyed the garden after Dorothy had died, nurturing the Birds of Paradise and the Agapanthus, the double delight roses and the Calla Lilies. She had lovingly planted her wildflowers each year in amongst the perennials, flowering shrubs, and bulbs, while their children grew, less like flowers than like weeds, and, one by one, left the swings and the sand box behind. They left the Sunday BBQ's and the sleepovers under the stars. They left the basketball hoop with its net shredded in the driveway. They left for medical schools and lawschool and art school. They left to make marriages, gardens, and children of their own. Now Dorothy had left him too.

Opening the door from the garage into the kitchen, Ralph was thankful to find the big old shaggy orange cat purring loudly, arching its back, flicking its bushy tail back and forth, and rubbing up against his leg. Custer had been Dorothy's cat, only putting up with Ralph for his mistress's sake. In recent months, Ralph and Custer had formed an alliance against loneliness and tactile deprivation. It was an amicable treaty, with each party grateful for the presence of the other.

Catching a glimpse of the message light blinking on the answering machine, Ralph tossed his keys on the kitchen counter, hit the play/rewind button, took out a can of Friskies turkey and giblets from the pantry. He opened the can while listening to the familiar voice of number-two daughter, singing out to him from the speaker.

"Hi daddy, it's Judy. Jack and I are calling from Positano. We're having a wonderful time here. Italy is awesome! From here, we'll be going back to Rome on Monday. Try you again from there. Hope you're O.K. Kisses. Bye."

She was still his baby. A recent graduate of Cal Arts, Judy, and her husband of one year were taking their delayed honeymoon in Italy before settling down to attend graduate school in New York. Ralph missed her so much it hurt. Judy, even more than the others, reminded him of her mother. He ached just thinking of Dorothy as he listened once more to the voice of his baby—of *their baby*.

The hot shower couldn't wash away the last twenty-four hours. It only dulled the pain of his throbbing muscles and diluted the tears. In the bedroom, Ralph found Custer staked out on top of the clean clothes he'd pulled from the closet and laid out on the bed.

"Sorry fella, gotta go again."

Ralph stroked the cat with tenderness and gave him a gentle shove.

CHAPTER 8

Interrogation at the Morgue

The Beverly Hills Police station, long ago housed in the older section of the Civic Center under the ornate gilded cupola of City Hall, had in recent years been relocated to the newly completed collection of archways, promenades and courtyards off Rexford Drive. After parking on the third level of the municipal lot and crossing the bridge to the second floor of the building, Claudine, Lucienne, and Kurt followed the signs displayed conspicuously about to help visitors find their way in and out of a monotonous maze of aqua and peach stucco.

Claudine glimpsed the tip of the building, the City Hall where she and Bernard had applied for their marriage license. As they walked through the double doors, she looked about, hoping to see Ralph. Instead, they were greeted by a series of monument-size frames that bound a collection of police department patches from every imaginable town in the country. Lucienne loitered before each one. The last place she wanted to go was straight on. She paused between Bemidji, Minnesota and Muskogee, Oklahoma to brush the hair from her forehead. Between Barstow, California and Bear's Skin Neck, Massachusetts she adjusted her jewelry. She stopped again to light a cigarette and continued to the wall-mounted ashtray, taking one last draw before putting it out.

Each colorful collage of badges functioned to reassure the public that the BHPD was linked in an endless and formidable chain of law enforcement agencies, crisscrossing the country. Clearly the message was: *Alfred's murderer can run, but he cannot hide from these brave men and women who defend the law of the land.* As they rounded the corner and approached the front desk, Detective Orloff jogged down the stairs behind them.

"Ladies, Kurt, I was hoping to intercept you. If you'll just come this way. I'll escort you downstairs."

Claudine waited outside the door marked *Morgue*. On the other side of that same door, Lucienne stood expressionless as the rubberized sheet was pulled back from her husband's face. Like most day-old corpses, Alfred's appeared characterless and smooth, a waxen, almost mannequin-like version of a once-breathing being. Its visage had borne lines and contours, smiles and frowns, the expressions of life. But not any longer. Lucienne stared for several moments, unwilling to pull away, as if hoping that he would reanimate, sit up and speak. After a while, she capitulated to reality.

"It is Alfred, of course. But he looks as if he has vacated the premises. He is not there, and yet this is his body."

She turned to Kurt, standing silently by her, one arm held out behind her back, poised to brace her from any possible fall.

"All the history, his arrogance, his charm, his elegance, it is all gone. It is as if it has leaked out with all that blood. You did say there was a good deal of blood, did you not, Detective?"

"Sorry to have to put you through this, Mrs. Merrill."

Ralph nodded to the technician standing by. He led the two away into a small room off the morgue. On a wooden table in the middle of the room lay a plastic bag filled with some small items: a watch, a gold wedding band, once wide but now smooth and narrowed with wear, a pair of scratched gold cufflinks, and a mother-of-pearl tie bar, assorted coins, a fine black Italian leather card case, and a money clip with a twenty-dollar bill visible on the outside of the sheaf of larger bills.

Lucienne had barely touched the bags when she recoiled. The cufflinks, tie bar, money clip and card case each marked a different occasion. All were gifts she'd given to her husband. The ring was a reminder of their long-gone and wildly romantic youth. Stoically, she diverted her gaze away from the table full of souvenirs and toward the detective's eyes.

"And where are his clothes?" she demanded despondently.

"I'm afraid those contain evidence. They'll be retained for the time being."

"Of course," Lucienne said, voice wavering and weary. "I suppose you have questions Mr. Orloff, or should I call you Detective Orloff?"

"No matter. I'll need a brief statement from you—from both of you actually, as to your whereabouts last evening between, say, five and six. And perhaps anything you may have to tell me about who might have had some motive for killing Doctor Merrill, any enemies he may have made over the years."

"But of course, Kurt and I will cooperate fully, won't you Kurt?" Lucienne asked, taking the young man's arm. "You see, Kurt knows many of our friends. He has taught their children to ride over the years. Even some of the parents have taken lessons with him. As to where I was between five and six last night," she paused and looked around for a place to sit. "I hope you don't mind."

"Please," Ralph gestured to a long maple bench flanked by two straight-backed chairs along one wall. "Why don't we have a seat over there."

Lucienne chose one of the chairs. She opened her purse, reached in, and withdrew a flat gold case, her initials engraved on the top. Flipping it open, she slipped out a long, mahogany brown Sherman cigarette. Placing it between painted lips, she looked into Ralph's eyes with yearning. On cue, he searched his pockets.

He produced a pack of matches and lit one. As he held it to her cigarette, he said, "There's no smoking in the Morgue."

"Thank you," she said, pausing to inhale. Then she sighed, "You see, we were to leave for the continent last night at eleven."

"Not to London?" Ralph asked with a note of surprise.

"Actually, we were to fly to London first. I intended to continue on to Paris by myself." Anticipating Ralph's next inquiry, Lucienne added, "You must understand, Detective Orloff. Alfred has his family and colleagues in London, many ties to the London Institute and The British Psycho-Analytical Society. That was where he trained, you know, at The London Institute of Psychoanalysis. His analyst, she's still there as well. He had his affairs to look after, while I of course had my own."

Ralph nodded.

"I do hope you understand," she went on. "It is a modern life we live. Lived, I mean. After all, we have, we had different interests." A single tear moved slowly down her cheek. "I was packing our bags in my room, when Daniel called around five-fifteen."

"Daniel?"

"*Oui*, Daniel Collins, Alfred's friend. Or I suppose you could say his protege. Alfred had trained him. They were quite close, so of course he called to say goodbye. I think he said something about covering Alfred's practice. I really cannot recall just now," she said, dragging in the smoke fiercely with her last words.

"So, you were on the phone with Doctor Collins from five-fifteen until . . ."

"No, no, we did not speak. He left a message on the answering machine. I did not care to take any calls at the time, so I simply let the machine pick up."

"So, you heard him leaving the message?"

"No. I only heard the message sometime later on, when I went into the kitchen to get a glass of wine."

"And do you recall what time that was?"

"Oh, perhaps around six or six-thirty. I remember thinking that Alfred would be home at any time, and so I noted down Daniel's call on the pad by the telephone rather than calling Alfred's office to tell him. Then I erased the message."

"Go on," Ralph coaxed.

"Well, after that I prepared some cheese and fruit to have with the fresh baguette I had baked that afternoon for a light snack when Alfred returned. We rarely eat a full meal in the evening. Especially when we are flying. Then I called Constance Manning."

"And she is . . .?"

"She owns the stallion we are breeding our mare to. Next week. Or, as soon as Fancy comes into her thirty-day heat. I wanted to remind Constance that Kurt would be trailering Fancy and her colt out to Santa Ynez without me, so that if she needed to talk to me about anything, we could take care of it over the telephone."

"And about what time was that?"

"I know it must have been between six-thirty and seven. You see, Constance said that the family was just sitting down to the table for supper, and she asked if she could call me back in a little while. I know that they dine around that time, and I can remember scolding myself for being so thoughtless. I have become rude in my old age," Lucienne said, laughing as she pronounced the words *old age*, as if to emphasize the absurdity of such a term being applied to anyone as youthful in appearance as herself.

"After that, I went to the stable. Kurt and I turned Fancy and her colt out in the arena for a time, just to allow them to stretch while we fed the others and cleaned and placed fresh bedding into their stalls." Glancing over at the younger man, who now seemed to be far off in his own thoughts, Lucienne asked, "Would you say that was about seven or so, Kurt *cheri*?"

Jerking his head around toward Lucienne's voice, Kurt replied. He seemed edgy, reluctant to be forced out of his contemplative state to join in the conversation. "Yes, Ma'am, that seems about right to me. I was just measuring the grain into the buckets when you came out. Before that, I'd been in teasing the mares."

"Teasing," Ralph repeated, wondering what Kurt had been so absorbed by in his thoughts. What had he been up to at the time of the murder?

"Yessir," Kurt confirmed.

"I brought out the stallion, The Major, that's Doc's horse. We call him The Major, but his registered name is *Majority of Juan*. That's because he's out of *Major's Mynah* and by *VF Don Juan*. That's VF for Ventura Farms, over in Hidden Valley, yaw know?"

"I see," Ralph said, although he didn't really quite understand what seemed to be some sort of horse breeders' jargon.

"Teasing is when I bring the stallion up to nuzzle a bit with each of the mares. I guess you could say that he whispers sweet nothings in their ears. That is, until they either squeal with delight and put their tails up over their backs, giving him the go-ahead, or they just turn tail and kick the barn door as if to say, 'not tonight, I have a headache.'"

Kurt chuckled. A juvenile enthusiasm returned to his voice as he continued to describe the mating rituals of Lucienne's elegant equines.

Lucienne, meanwhile, seemed irritated. "This is routine in the barn in the evenings," she said. "When we have mares with us for breeding, or when we are preparing to send one of ours out to be bred elsewhere, like our Fancy."

Ralph made a mental note of Lucienne's defensive posture and looked back at Kurt.

"So, you were in the barn between five and six?"

"Yep, that's right," Kurt confirmed.

"Anyone see you there during that time?"

"No one but the horses, the barn cats, and of course there's Fred. Guess you could call it a shaggy-dog story."

"Really, Detective Orloff," Lucienne protested. "Are you certain that this is necessary? You cannot possibly think Kurt would harm a hair on Alfred's head. He was like a father to the boy."

"Do you play chess, Mrs. Merrill?" Ralph asked, recalling the antique French pewter set wedged into the bookcase in Alfred's consulting room.

"Yes. But what could that have to do with anything?" she asked, half exasperated, half intrigued.

"Solving a crime is something like playing chess. It's important to know where all the pieces on the chessboard are. One missing piece can throw the whole game off."

"I sure don't wanna be the burr underneath your saddle, Detective," Kurt said. "I don't mean to be the one to throw you off your game. I sure wish I had more information to give you, but I don't." He shrugged his broad shoulders.

"I think I have all of the information I need for the time being," Ralph said, closing the notepad and sliding his pencil over his right ear. "Of course, I'll be getting back to you, Mrs. Merrill. After I go through the Doctor's files." Ralph ushered the two of them out to where Claudine was waiting. "Do you need me to show you out of the building?"

"No, no. I think we can find the car," Lucienne said, as they reached Claudine, already out of her seat and moving toward them.

"I will see you later, dearest Claudine."

"Of course. Kurt, look after Lucienne, will you," Claudine implored, squeezing his hand with affection.

CHAPTER 9

The Game's Afoot

Ralph supported Claudine's elbow, guiding her through the building toward the lot where his car was parked. She seemed deep in thought. Passing through several doors until they finally reached the Centurion, he couldn't help but wonder what occupied her thoughts. Before he could ask, she turned to him as he opened the car door. It was as if she could read his mind.

"Please do not think badly of Lucienne," she said. "I know how it might look to you. But you must understand that she is in a massive state of denial. She may even appear to be cold and unaffected by Alfred's death. But, in spite of everything, she loved him and was always quite dedicated to him in her own way."

Ralph was utterly captured by this woman's look, by the proximity of her, by her scent. Even more than that, he felt seized by her words, which seemed to reveal an acute capacity for caring and tuning in. He closed the car door and walked to the driver's side, took a deep breath, and seated himself behind the wheel. He hesitated to start the car. After a long pause, he turned toward Claudine.

"I'll tell you what's so disturbing for me," he said. After another deep breath, he was all the more certain that he could confide in her. "You see, I just lost my wife a few months ago. I remember how I reacted to her death. So, if you ask me, that is one cold cookie."

Claudine looked stung. Ralph tried to soften what might, in fact, have been too harsh. "You don't have to worry," he said gently. "Your friend is far from number one on my list of suspects. In fact, I don't even have a list yet. Let's see what else we can turn up in this case." Ralph started the engine and drove off toward Roxbury.

He had begun to brood on the possibility that his attraction to her might, in fact, make it harder rather than easier to solve the case, when she suddenly asked, "How do you proceed in an investigation like this, Detective?"

He shrugged. "From the evidence. From questioning the relevant people." He paused, then added, "And from intuition—which is hardly infallible."

"What, if anything, *is* infallible, in your experience?"

"Dreams."

Claudine practically recoiled in surprise. She laughed. "Dreams? That is quite possibly the last answer I would have expected to hear from a cool, hardened, unemotional hunter-of-thieves-and-murderers like yourself."

"All the same, dreams are what I trust," he reiterated with a broad grin. "Why are you surprised? I would think that a psychoanalyst would also believe that dreams are the most reliable access to the unconscious. What really goes on inside a person's mind is displayed in his dreams."

"*Bien sûr.* That is true. But I *am* a psychoanalyst. You're a police detective. How is it that you come to value dreams so?"

Now Ralph was the one laughing. "It's really simple. When I was consulting with Doctor Merrill years ago, I discovered that my dreams contained lots of stored observations I'd made during the day without quite being aware of them. Which is to say, *unconsciously.* Clues, pieces of the puzzle that every crime presents, pieces that don't fit together neatly in any given day of an investigation are unwittingly pushed out of awareness and are stored in the back of the mind. I found out that, in my dreams, I do some of my best thinking, combining, and re-combining these clues until they form some sort of a coherent pattern.

"I discovered that, at least in dreams, my intuition is relatively uninhibited. Things that are unthinkable in waking life are contemplated unconsciously. Of course, these things are *disguised* when they're revealed to me in dreams. I think you call that the manifest content of the dream, right? Guess you could say I learned the trick of how dream analysis works to penetrate these disguises, and the way it helps to reveal the solution to the puzzle of the crime. The way I look at it, it's as if by teasing out the elements of my personal past, I get a clearer image of the present. By weeding out the people, places and events that obscure my perception of events in the present, I can get a much clearer view of the case I'm trying to solve."

"So that is the secret of your success, is it, *Mr. Holmes*?"

"Elementary, my dear Doctor Ingersoll." He added, "You see, you weren't so off-base when you suggested that we're both detectives."

"I suppose not. However, it appears that I may also have made an erroneous distinction between us. It seems we both investigate the *internal* mystery as a way of de-mystifying the external state of affairs, the truth. What irony that Alfred should have been a major contributor to the development of a technique that is useful in the investigation into his own death—that he might be aiding the police, *après coup*, in the pursuit of his own murderer."

"I suppose some would call it *Karma*," Ralph said.

"Karma indeed. I wonder if there may be a good many aspects of this case that could fall under that heading."

"Such as?"

"Oh, I didn't have anything specific in mind. It's only that . . ." Claudine paused for a moment, then reaching across the wide bench seat to find Ralph's hand, caressing it gently. "I think you are about to learn that Alfred was quite a complex man."

They pulled up to the curb just as a somewhat slight and slim bearded man approached the Roxbury building. He wore gray slacks, a pale blue shirt, a conservatively striped tie, and a navy-blue blazer. He looked like he was in a rush. As he swung open the door he caught sight of them getting out the car. Holding the door with a scant smile, he picked up a morning paper from the stack by the door and shaded his eyes from the too-bright sun.

"Claudine, I thought you left last night for Geneva," he said. "Don't tell me you missed your flight." He walked with them inside, toward the elevator.

"No, Daniel. I'm afraid it's not as simple as that," Claudine replied. "Daniel, this is Detective Ralph Orloff of the Beverly Hills Police Department. Detective, this is Doctor Daniel Collins."

Collins right eye began twitching with discomfort. "Police? Anything the matter? I hope you haven't been robbed or . . . ."

"No, Daniel. I'm afraid it is much more serious than that. It's about Alfred." Claudine spoke gingerly as they entered the elevator, the door sliding closed behind them. "You've not heard or read the news yet?"

"Alfred was robbed?"

"Worse than that, Daniel. More than you could imagine. Alfred has been murdered."

"What? Murdered—"

The word stuck like a bone in Collins' throat. His whole face blanched and tears instantly appeared. He closed his eyes and shook his head, as if to erase what he'd just heard. When he opened them once more, it almost seemed that he was attempting to restart the conversation, hoping Claudine might say something else. "You can't mean it."

"It's true, Daniel. Alfred was killed last night in his consulting room. That is why I am here with the police, not in Geneva."

As the elevator reached the fourth floor, Claudine took the younger man's clammy hand in hers, leading him down the hallway. His eyes, fixed and expressionless, spoke without a word. He was in shock. When they reached his office, Claudine took his keys from his hand and unlocked his door. He stood motionless.

"Are you here to see a patient or a supervisee?" Claudine asked.

"Yes. One of the second-year candidates, Susan Rees. She's coming for supervision at ten," Daniel spoke in a monotone, eyes now opaque. "And after Susan, I have a group from the Neuro-Psychiatric Institute," he muttered. "I can cancel them. Except for Susan. She'll be on her way already." Reeling, Collins paused. "I don't know if I can see her." He shook his head. "Can't believe it. That's why he never called me back last night." Collins crumbled over the threshold and turned to Claudine. "Where will you be if I need you?"

"We will be right up the hall, looking through some of Alfred's things," Claudine said. "Just come when you are finished, knock on the door. Do you think that you'll be alright when Susan comes, or would you like me to stay and wait for her?"

"I'll be O.K." After another gap, Collins turned his ashen face toward Claudine. "Shit. No, I won't," he sputtered. "How the fuck can I be okay? You know what he was to me. Damn it to hell," he stammered, dragging his body inside the suite. He closed the door with effort, as if it weighed a ton.

"Was Alfred his analyst?" Ralph asked. When Claudette nodded, he said, "No wonder he was wiped out by the news"

"Yes. Poor Daniel. They were so very close."

"But I thought I heard Lucienne mention that Collins had been *trained* by him."

"Yes, well that can be a bit confusing to an outsider. I shall try to explain."

Claudine unlocked her door and led Ralph into her own consulting room.

"When we enroll in the Institute to become analysts, along with several years of seminars and analyzing patients under supervision, each candidate must undergo his or her own personal analysis."

"Just how long does that usually go on?"

"It varies somewhat, depending upon the candidate, of course, but it's not unusual these days for a training analysis to last throughout the training or even beyond certification, often eight to ten years. Sometimes much more."

"That long, huh?"

"Frequently. After all, we know a great deal more about the human mind today than they did in Freud's time, and our technique has improved as well."

"So, the training analyst determines how much is enough?" Ralph asked.

"Actually, the requirement is that the length be to the mutual satisfaction of both the analyst and the analysand. It is between doctor and patient. It lasts until each is convinced that the candidate has sufficiently become familiarized with his own experiences of early and later childhood, and with the fantasies and myths about these stages of life that he or she has created and kept in the unconscious. These personal themes, around which the analyst organizes experiences, are basic to the ways he or she will perceive and make meaning of their patients' infantile and childhood happenings."

"Sounds complex," Ralph said.

"It is. At the very least, we must become consciously aware of those organizing principles in ourselves. This is one of the main goals of the training analysis."

"So Collins was analyzed by Merrill during his training?"

"Yes, he was. And now, after some years, Daniel has himself earned the privilege of being a senior analyst, training new candidates in the Institute. He had also maintained a very close, collegial relationship with Alfred during the years since the termination of his own analysis. They had served on committees together and collaborated on scientific panels. It's a bit, shall we say, unusual, but they socialized a good deal as well. Daniel's children take riding lessons from Kurt. The whole family spends quite a bit of time with Alfred and Lucienne."

"I see. So, in a manner of speaking, Collins is heir to Alfred's professional throne."

Claudine paused before answering, "That is one way to put it, yes."

The reality of Alfred's death reasserted itself the moment they entered the room. In spite of the windows that Ralph had left open earlier that morning, the unmistakable odor of the outrage that had occurred on the previous evening was inescapable. The lingering stench, along with the vision of chalk marks on the couch and the remainders of the powder from the finger printing process, all wrapped up in a neat package with an official yellow crime-scene ribbon, underscored the task at hand.

"Whew!" Ralph sighed. "I'll never get used to the scent of death, if I live to be a hundred. Can't be too pleasant for you, either. We'll try to make it short.," He turned away from her and walked over to the window. A tide of nausea suddenly threatened to pull him under. It wasn't just the odor.

Claudine seemed to note his discomfort. "This murder is anything but just another case for you," she said. "Why don't we take Alfred's files and his appointment book into my office? This room is a mess, and it might be difficult for us to work here. Surely it contains many intimate, even sacred memories for you. I can only imagine what you must have felt, seeing him lying there. Not to mention all the people moving about here last night."

"It felt like an invasion of my privacy. I'll get over it." He looked away, attempting to minimize the mental pain. In its place, a physical symptom, a lump, formed in his throat.

"Then it's settled," she said. "We shall work in my room. Let me make us some coffee . . ." She disappeared into the kitchen. "—or would you prefer tea?"

"Coffee, please."

Moving toward the bookcases, he reached out to run his fingers over each object tucked between the familiar volumes of Freud and Klein: a pre-Columbian figure, its erect member poking out at a perfect right angle to its torso, a piece of rough-cut stone out of which a hand emerged holding the naked figures of a man and woman embracing; a bronze bull, too well-hung; a pewter chess set with figures straight out of a Tolkien fantasy; a bronze statuette of a mother with her infant at the breast; an urn filled with pale pastel *potpourri,* which had long ago lost its scent—they were all, to Ralph, familiar artifacts.

Ralph caught himself thinking of his personal loss and felt a touch of shame. He needed a new topic. He crossed the hall toward the kitchen. "Besides the patients he treated," he said, "what about the others?"

"Did you say others?"

"You know, people he knew in the Institute? Students, supervisees, colleagues . . ." As he admired the grace with which Claudine made the coffee, he asked, "Did he have any enemies that you are aware of?"

She stopped what she doing and looked at him. "Of course, I will try to be as helpful to you as I can. But first I must be certain that you understand one thing about the work we do."

"What's that?"

"The passions experienced in the therapeutic relationship between the analyst and patient in the training situation, in the transference, unfortunately can and do leak out of the consulting room. They may inevitably find expression in the politics of the institute and in the analytic society. Just moments ago, you yourself experienced the fragility of the boundaries of the analytic process and its setting."

Ralph winced. "You mean that thing just now with Collins? Yeah, I see what you mean. Quite a powerful case of sibling rivalry on my part. And with a man I'd barely met. I'll admit, I was blown away by the extent of my jealousy and resentment toward the poor guy."

"I hope you will keep that experience in mind when I tell you that there existed passions, both love and hatred, between Alfred and others of our group. That is not to say that any one of them would have acted on their passions. *We also cannot be certain that they did not act on them.* Perhaps nothing can be all black."

"Except my coffee," he said, as she poured.

CHAPTER 10

Accounts of Conflict and Conflicting Accounts

Claudine and Ralph spent much of that day compiling lists of names, phone numbers, and addresses. Alfred had developed many noteworthy relationships with professionals in the analytic community, with those of his own society as well as others in America and abroad. Ralph soon came to learn all about the politics of psychoanalysis in Los Angeles and the conflicts that had their roots in Great Britain.

"You should know that there are four major internationally accredited psychoanalytic training institutes in Los Angeles," Claudine said.

"Independent of one another?"

"In a way, yes. Although there are strong personal and professional ties between individuals from so-called competitive institutes. Of course, there are scientific collaborations as well. The history of psychoanalysis in this city is such that many analysts who trained at one institute are related, through their training analysts or supervisors, to those in other groups."

"Cliques?"

"Well, you might say *inbred* groups of analysts and their analysands. They refer patients to one another and consider themselves to be *keepers of the faith* for a given theoretical orientation. The situation in Los Angeles in the late sixties through the seventies actually evolved out of a philosophical conflict that began in London during World War II. Unfortunately, that same conflict is being re-enacted in our small community, even today."

"Are you referring to the feud between Freud's daughter and Melanie Klein? I knew Alfred was very high on Klein. I once attended one of his public lectures, where he talked about her work."

"So, you know something about this."

"Very little."

"Both women immigrated to England from Europe. Klein came from Berlin in the late twenties and Anna Freud from Vienna with her father in 1938. Both women were pioneers in child analysis. Each felt she had earned the right to carry the torch for Freud."

"Speaking of sibling rivalry! Did Freud take sides?"

"Never. In the last year of his life, he stood by and observed as one of the most heated disputes in the history of psychology took quite a nasty turn just before he died."

"What was it all about?"

"The battle was fought over matters of curriculum, what was to be taught as psychoanalysis. Mrs. Klein asserted her observations and convictions based upon her method of child analysis. The interpretation of the play of children within a therapeutic setting was central to Klein's work. She proposed that child's play was equivalent to the verbal associations and dreams of adults. Ms. Freud, on the contrary, insisted that certain parameters of an educational nature such as discipline, guidance, and instruction, were necessary elements in the treatment of children. This resulted in a difference in Anna Freud's technique, and as one would expect, to observations of a different level of development, and often of a contradictory nature from those made by Mrs. Klein. For example, where Anna Freud would use a a pedagogic approach to her work with children, and only after 4-6 years of age, assuming a good-enough infancy. Klein observed that a good-enough infancy could not be taken for granted, that infantile neurosis can begin even before birth and certainly in earliest infancy, and that the interpretation of infantile unconscious fantasies in the transference relationship with the analyst was not only possible, but essential.

"It's a wonder anyone in London even noticed the blitz," Ralph said.

"For some, the Germans were a remote threat compared with the enemy in their midst. With adherents and opponents making their arguments about what psychoanalysis was and what it was not, about how it should be taught and by whom, the strife transcended the war. Even under cover of scientific camouflage, the attacks and counter-attacks launched by each woman and her army of supporters against the other in the public forum of the meetings of the British Society had the unmistakable flavor of personal polemic."

"How did they finally settle their differences?"

"The *gentlewoman's agreement*, it was called. The training program of the Institute in London was re-organized, an unprecedented compromise. Three separate training tracks were established. There was the Anna Freudian Group, also known as the Freudian Group; the Kleinian Group, sometimes referred to as the English School; and a group that came to be known as the Middle School, or the Independents, which was made up largely of those analysts who refrained from allying themselves with either school, but who wished to reserve the right to learn from both."

"And how did this play here in the States?"

"After the war, the first psychoanalytic society and institute in Los Angeles was established by a small group of local intellectuals under the tutelage of some refugees, mostly from Austria and Germany. These analysts were men and women who had crossed the

Atlantic with the help of one American in particular, a psychologist who had received his analytic experience in Vienna with Sigmund Freud, and who, much later on, returned to England for a second analysis with Anna."

"Would that be David Brunswick? I heard they called him *Affidavit Brunswick* because he sponsored so many refugees."

Claudine raised an eyebrow.

Ralph smiled broadly. He'd impressed her. "A friend of mine was in treatment with Brunswick before he died," Ralph said. "Nice guy, I've been told. I also heard that the L.A. Institute split in the fifties."

"Ironically, after a bitter conflict over medical supremacy in the field. The new institute and society distinguished itself for what was called 'medical psychoanalysis.' Some said that the issue of whether one should be a medical doctor in order to be trained in the practice of analysis was a *red herring*. The real issue was economic, just as it had been in London in the forties."

"Makes sense. Whoever has the power over matters of training has the most work. It always boils down to money."

"But the cost to our profession was dear," Claudine said. "Analysts and candidates had to choose sides between the old Viennese analysts, most of whom were not medical doctors, and their descendants, the medical analysts, most of whom were American psychiatrists."

"Did either side win? Or lose?"

"Well, after some initial conflict, there was a relatively peaceful period of coexistence between the two societies. During the turbulent fifties and early sixties, many of the English School analysts from London came to give seminars and papers, mostly to private groups of analysts who were dissatisfied with the work, with the results they were getting. But it was not until the late sixties that a few London Kleinians agreed to move to Los Angeles at the urging of this group, some from each of the two Los Angeles-based institutes, who had been until then learning underground."

"What precipitated the immigration? Was Alfred in that group?" Ralph asked.

"There were a number of relatively recently graduated members of both societies who had become even more dissatisfied with the tools afforded them by their restricted trainings in what were then typical American institutes dominated by the teachings of Anna Freud, not her father. Her technique centered itself around the analysis of the *defenses* and paid little attention to the primitive *anxieties* that necessitated their deployment. These younger analysts, and even some of the elders, were dissatisfied with the progress their patients were making, as well as with the results of their own personal analyses. They resorted to underground independent study groups outside their institutes. These study groups were devoted to learning about the extension of Freud's ideas, particularly those evolving out of Melanie Klein's work with children, and her immediate followers' experience treating psychotic adults. Klein's work was concerned with the analysis of elemental unconscious fantasies and the forms of anxiety that these provoked. Many analysts in Los Angeles were excited and encouraged by what they were learning, by the ways in which these new ideas seemed to enhance and add additional dimensions to their work. Their patients were benefitting, which made their work gratifying "

"Sounds exciting."

"It was invigorating. After a time, they wanted more. Many local analysts wished to be re-analyzed by Kleinians. This meant at least a temporary relocation by some of the members of the British Society."

"So, Alfred was among the pioneers from across the pond?"

"Yes. He was the junior member to come over. There were others more senior and very well known, like Wilfred Bion."

"I once read that he had analyzed Samuel Beckett."

Claudine smiled. "I'm impressed, Detective!"

He looked cool. "We're not all Joe Friday."

"Who?"

Now Ralph smiled. "Never mind. So, what happened next?"

"Soon there was another intense power struggle in Los Angeles. Anna Freud wielded her power through her protégés in this country. Her chief standard bearer was a famous and powerful man, the analyst to such stars as Marilyn Monroe. And many American Kleinians became casualties of that war. They were denied supervising and training-analyst status and were even barred from teaching courses in their own institutes."

Ralph looked pensive. "You know," he said carefully, "this is not exactly something you expect to hear, in the history of what's supposed to be a science."

To his surprise, she laughed. "Oh, that's not true at all! Sciences are always split by rival theories. In physics, today, one school of thought takes string theory very seriously, while another insists that it's not only not true, but it's not even science. What is the phrase? That it's 'not even wrong.'"

He smiled. "Now *I'm* impressed, Doctor."

"Good. We're even."

He tried to conceal his delight, and thought he did a fairly good job of it. "So what happened next?" he said.

"Another new institute was born. The American Kleinian analysts eventually accepted an invitation to teach and train at a new institute. Unfortunately, these days, another power struggle threatens an irreparable split. Alfred was a key figure in the debate, sometimes referred to as the Paleo-Kleinians versus the Neo-Kleinians." She added, "And he was on . . . let us say, on tense terms, with some of the members of the group he opposed."

"Anyone I should be focusing on?"

"John Goldman and Giancarlo Giachinni," Claudine spoke hesitantly, and with discomfort. Before she could say anymore, they heard a knock on the exit door.

Daniel Collins looked even worse than when Claudine and Ralph had seen him to his office some hours before. His tie was loosened, he'd shed his blazer, and his face, which had been drawn and chalky when he'd first heard the news, was now flushed, swollen and distorted. His bulbous nose and narrowed eyes were red and puffy. He'd been weeping and possibly drinking too much. He stumbled through the door with a half-full glass of what looked like scotch clutched in his left hand.

"I just couldn't tolerate being alone anymore. It's hit the papers, you know," Collins said, thrusting a rolled-up section of the *Los Angeles Times* at Claudine, staggering past her through the inner hallway, and stumbling toward Merrill's consulting room.

Claudine glanced at the headline. *Couch-Canyon Cut-Throat Sought, BHPD Investigation Underway*

Barely upright on his unsteady pins in the doorway of Alfred's room, Collins leaned against the wooden jamb. Gulping down the remainder of his drink, he burst into tears.

Claudine went to his aid. "Come, Daniel. Come away. Just come and sit down in here."

She led her younger colleague out of Merrill's office and into her own. When she released him, he nearly crumbled into a large, overstuffed club chair upholstered in the same tapestry fabric as her couch. Collins' head dropped like a rock onto fists supported on wobbly knees.

Ralph found it increasingly difficult to sustain his previous resentment for Collins. He now eyed the broken man whose pain resonated with his own.

"They said he was found with his throat cut," Daniel sobbed, looking to each of them for rebuttal.

None was forthcoming. "Then it's true!" he cried and looked to the detective. "Oh fuck, do you know who did it?"

"We've only just begun our investigation, Doctor," Ralph said. "I'm sorry to have to ask this, but anything you might know that could be of help would be appreciated. I take it you were close to Doctor Merrill. And your office is just down the hall. Maybe you saw or heard something or someone unusual—say between four-thirty and six-thirty last evening?"

"I was with patients all afternoon; I mean until five-forty-five. Michelle, my wife, she and I had a meeting with a decorator at the house at six. I left the office almost immediately. Certainly a few minutes before five. I didn't run into anyone leaving the floor. I took the stairs down and went out the back to my car."

"That's all you remember. Nothing else?"

"No, nothing. Wait. I did see a car parked in the lot that caught my eye. I thought it odd that his car should be here. That old Vet, the yellow one that belongs to John, John Goldman?"

Goldman. Claudine had mentioned him as an adversary of Merrill's. Ralph decided to play dumb.

"And who's he?"

"John and his wife Sheila were old friends of the Merrill's. That is until recently, when Alfred stood up at a scientific meeting and launched a thinly veiled attack on some of John's ideas. Sometime after that, a few of us overheard John say that Alfred was an extinct breed of dinosaur who hadn't enough presence of mind, self-respect, or decency to just lay down on his couch and die. You were there, Claudine. You heard him!"

"Dan," Claudine said carefully. "That was said off the record and in a certain state of mind. I'm sure he didn't mean it."

"You don't believe that do you? He may have waited until after the meeting, but he meant for us to hear. For Alfred to hear, too. He wanted to hurt him."

"So, there was active friction between the two men," Ralph said.

"I'll say." Collins sounded irate. "Maybe you should go ask John what he was doing in the building last evening when Alfred was murdered."

"Daniel," Claudine said. "You really cannot possibly be thinking that John had anything to do with Alfred's death . . ."

"And why the hell not, Claudine? He's wanted to slit Alfred's throat for years. Who's to say he didn't finally act out his fantasy, once and for all? What else would he be here for, anyway?"

"Daniel, you are upset and not thinking clearly. There are many of us here in the building. I am certain there must be another explanation for John's car being parked in the lot."

Ralph intervened. "Doctor Collins, we've been compiling a list of people who knew the deceased," he said. "I'll be talking to everyone sooner or later. If you can think of anything more you'd like to say, please don't hesitate to contact me at this number." Ralph extended his card to the disheveled man.

Collins took it, rose unsteadily, and shuffled toward the door. Both Claudine and Ralph followed.

Collins turned. "I suppose you're right," he said. "I should go home to Michelle. Have you seen Lucienne? Is she alright?"

"Yes, I saw her this morning before we came here, "Claudine said. "Kurt is with her. Perhaps you may wish to call her. She might need some help with the funeral arrangements. And perhaps you may wish to take a taxi."

"Right. I'll do that. Good-bye Claudine, and thank you," he said, kissing her on both cheeks.

"Good-bye, Daniel." she said. As the door closed she rolled her eyes.

"As you can see, we analysts are a complex species. Now, shall we return to our task?"

"We never left it. Suppose you tell me something more about John Goldman. Why do *you* think he was here?"

"Actually, I . . . I cannot say," Claudine replied awkwardly.

"Any guesses?"

"I'm sorry, really. It seems I cannot even offer you a hint. But we could return to deciphering the hieroglyphics in Alfred's journal."

"I had a feeling we'd run into this sooner or later. It has to do with confidentiality, doesn't it?"

"I'm afraid so."

"Don't get me wrong," he smiled. "As a patient I'm grateful to hear that the laws of confidentiality and the principle of patient privacy is not just so much lip service. But as a cop trying to do my job, your impeccable ethics constitute a pain in the a . . . uh . . . er . . . an impediment to this investigation."

"Yes. Well, then, how shall we proceed?"

With a sigh, Ralph gave up the chase, regaining his good humor. "Why, discreetly of course, Madame."

Heads together, they paged through Merrill's appointment book, stopping at the day of the murder.

"O.K." Ralph said. He pointed at an entry. "What's this mean? '*Michael-canceled OT.*'"

"It probably refers to the patient, or perhaps a supervisee who is ordinarily seen at five-ten on Friday. You see here . . ." Claudine flipped back to January. "The name appears throughout the year in this same time slot. And at the same time on Tuesday, Wednesday, and Thursday."

"But this Friday he canceled. So, what's the *OT*?"

"Out-of-town might be a reasonable speculation. Perhaps a reminder Alfred made for himself about the reason for the cancellation just in case a pattern of absences should emerge that might have some meaning in the transference. There are often subtle and indirect communications embedded in a patient's behavior, or in the deep structure of the language. If it should prove later to be a part of a larger pattern of behavior, which conveys meaning from the analysand to his analyst, it would be a significant notation with some clinical value."

"I see. So Michael may have been out of town on this day. Then again, maybe he just told Alfred that, to establish an alibi for murder." He looked at Claudine. "Do we have the addresses and phone numbers for each of these patients?"

"Yes, they are all here in the back of the book. Any of the patients seen thus far this year."

Claudine reached over to show Ralph the directory. He got a whiff of her perfume. *Or was it perfume?* Could be it was just her own natural fragrance? He ordered himself to cut it out—at least as long as the case was open.

"I think we can get started, then," he said. He rose and put some distance between them, standing by the open window so he could think more clearly. "Now, if this were a normal procedure, I mean in the event of the death of an analyst by natural causes, wouldn't you contact his patients to inform them, even though they've probably all read about it by now? Just to offer to see them, or to arrange for a referral if needed. Maybe reaching out to somehow soften the blow? Would that be the normal procedure?"

"This is the first time I have had to deal with something like this. I'm not exactly certain that you would call me an expert, but I suppose what you suggest is very near to what I had in mind." She pursed her lips. "Of course, many of Alfred's patients are students or candidates at the Institute. They know one another, which allows for an added measure of support. And, of course, they would not be so much in need of a referral as a non-professional patient—for example, someone like yourself." Claudine looked deep into Ralph's eyes. "What about you, Detective Orloff? It seems to me that you may be carrying quite a burden yourself. Perhaps you have a need to talk to someone?"

Ralph was fixed by her gaze, as if the distance he'd just placed between them had suddenly vanished.

"I am not suggesting myself, of course," Claudine added. "But perhaps one of my colleagues could be of service to you during this time."

Ralph paused, temporarily speechless. What Claudine had said reminded him of how, in almost the same way and in nearly that same tone of voice, Dorothy had suggested that he might need to talk to someone. That someone had turned out to be Doctor Alfred Merrill.

"I might," he said. "I'll get back to you about it."

That night, Orloff had a dream.

He's in a house, or maybe it's a restaurant. He's stopped to have lunch at a diner while driving around the city investigating the murder. He's with Dorothy. There's a tiger or a lion outside, but they're safe. He notices other people are entering the diner. The windows and doors are ajar, and the animals get inside too. Ralph and Dorothy are attacked and are about to be eaten alive.

Ralph awakened for a moment, turned over, and went back to sleep. The dream began again.

He remembers what has gone on before, although Dorothy doesn't seem to remember a thing. He realizes that he must conceal what he knows from everyone. He must trick people so that they can't expose him again to the dangerous wild animals. Ralph and Dorothy meet a couple they know. Ralph becomes evasive with them when they suggest he and Dorothy join them for lunch.

This time Ralph barricades himself and Dorothy inside the restaurant with the doors and windows boarded up. He keeps vigil, barring all who might place them in jeopardy. He's certain that the others have been attacked and are dying outside. He hears their screams. But Ralph doesn't dare give the others sanctuary, or else he and Dorothy will be killed again. The others keep ringing the bell outside to get Ralph to let them in, but Ralph yells, "No, no, go away ... no, no. . . ."

The shrill ring of the alarm saved him.

Shaken, he crawled out of bed and headed to the bathroom to splash some cold water on the nightmare. On the way, he passed Dorothy's dressing table, her perfumes still arranged on the mirrored tray. He recalled the scent of Claudine's perfume, the feelings he'd had when he was with her that afternoon. There was that sense of her as a woman, not just an analyst. It was the same impression he had when they had been together in his car, and again when she was making coffee.

He turned on the shower and stepped in. The cold spray felt necessary, therapeutic.

Stay cool, strong.

There was also his awareness of Claudine the therapist. It generated a sense—that he normally only felt in relationships of many years' duration—that she *knew* him. He had felt it when, in the car, Claudine had tapped into his feelings, his inner thoughts about Lucienne's callousness, and later when she had picked up on his need to talk about himself.

I am having a reaction to this case, he told himself. *The dream attests to that, alright. It's as if the dream is warning that there are dangerous feelings just outside my awareness, emotions that threaten to consume me.*

Ralph scrubbed his back, as if to erase the forbidden images. *What about Dorothy in the dream? <u>Was</u> it Dorothy? Or was it Dorothy in the first dream and someone else in the re-write of the dream? Is it my capacity for feeling strongly about a woman like Claudine that threatens to overwhelm me? It's dangerous enough to have loved a woman so deeply even once in a lifetime. Do I dare allow such feelings to enter my heart and mind again?*

Stepping out of the shower, Ralph rubbed his face dry, blotting out the thoughts as well. He glanced at the door to the bathroom. He'd locked it without thinking. As he wrapped himself in the towel, the thoughts and images returned.

Who are those people I sacrifice while I secure myself behind locked doors? Have I been pushing my children away since Dorothy's death? What about Alfred's children, his orphaned patients, people like myself who depended on him to protect and shelter us from harm? Am I the one who's been locked out of that shelter? Am I left helpless in the face of a devouring animal? Is that animal my grief about the loss of my wife and the love of my life, Dorothy?

By contacting Merrill after Dorothy's death, had Ralph once again turned from the lost mother, the mother of his infancy, toward his second father, only to lose that father as well? Ralph recalled the death of his own parents a dozen years apart—first his father's death from tuberculosis, precipitated by chronic alcoholism.

The image of Daniel Collins, intoxicated with grief and whiskey, flashed before his mind's eye. Ralph's father drank because he felt guilty. Ralph's mother was forever accusing his father of trying to kill her with financial worry, with jealousy for another woman in his life, and with his incessant conflicts and competitions with *her* son, Ralph.

He wondered why the hell he was having these associations to the dreams. The wild animals at the door, were these perhaps his suspicions about Daniel Collins, that he was reluctant to allow into consciousness? Suspicions about all the Daniel Collinses in the city? What would he discover about the son and the father, about himself and Alfred Merrill?

Ralph was compelled to think about the dream, but even as the thoughts washed over him, he had caught himself attempting to rinse them away as he showered, to rub them out as he toweled off. His desire to bring his doubts and fears out into the open was strong, even as he plotted to cover them up while he dressed.

In his dark blue cotton shirt, white linen sport coat, French-blue slacks, white loafers and light blue-and-white paisley tie, the cover-up prevailed. Ralph's thoughts grew lighter in color and less weighty. He felt better. And he looked sharp—sharper than usual. His five-foot ten-inch wiry build had remained hard and trim over the years. He was proud of this old body. It had never once failed to earn him the five percent annual fitness bonus.

In the kitchen Ralph drank his coffee, only briefly glancing at the article about Alfred's murder in the California section of the Times. Custer sat on the front page.

Today, Ralph would meet once again with Claudine. He had many questions and hoped she could give him some answers. When he'd left her late on Saturday afternoon, she'd already begun the task of contacting each of Alfred's patients by telephone. Ralph had returned to his own office at police headquarters to begin setting up interviews with various members of the analytic society. He'd split the list with Ben and, after several busy signals and nearly as many encounters with answering machines, his first successful contact was with John Goldman.

"Yes, Detective Orloff, we read all about it in the papers early this morning," Goldman said. "And the telephone hasn't stopped ringing since ten. We're all in shock, as you can well imagine. How can we help?"

"We'll need to meet as soon as possible. You could come down here to headquarters or I can come to you, if you prefer."

"Of course, I'll be as cooperative as I can, but if you could come here it would be more convenient for me and maybe even more productive for you. You see, I'm waiting for my wife to return home, and she might be able to help out, too. She's gone over to the Harrington's house. They live pretty close by. I'm sure they must be on your list as well. June and Bill Harrington? We all knew Alfred very well and . . . ." Goldman trailed off, as if he realized that his voice was growing less and less professional, more emotional.

"Yes," Ralph said. "I agree, it'll work out best if I come to your Rodeo Drive address. I have a few more calls to make. Then I'll be right over. I'll try to make it short."

Just a few more calls.

Ralph took another look at the list. The Harringtons were next, and he might be able to arrange a meeting with them after interviewing the Goldmans, since they lived nearby. He wondered why Sheila Goldman had gone to the Harringtons. Could it be that one or both had been in analysis with Alfred and, like Collins, needed someone to turn to.

Or it might be the beginning of a cover-up.

There was the issue of the Goldmans' Corvette, parked in the lot behind the building in which Merrill had been murdered. There was Collins' report of vituperative exchanges between John Goldman and the victim. Ralph made these notes to himself, to be filed in the back of his mind.

Skipping over Ingersoll, the next name on the list was Doctor Dahlia Jacobs. From the address it looked like Doctor Jacobs, who lived on South Bedford Drive, was right around the corner from the others, and only a few blocks from Doctor Giancarlo Giacchini, someone Ralph had tried to reach, but whose line had been busy—unusual in these days of the ubiquitous call-waiting.

After arranging to stop by the Harrington home right after the Goldmans', and finding a nervous but cooperative Dahlia Jacobs, at home for the rest of the day and evening, Ralph finally got through to Giacchini.

"*Pronto*," greeted the robust baritone on the other end of the line.

Ralph recalled Claudine mentioning three things about Doctor Giacchini. He had originally come from the Italian Society in Rome, where he had been trained, just a few years after Merrill had immigrated from England. Second, he was among the honorable opposition to Merrill in matters *scientific*. And last but not least, he pronounced his name like the squash.

"Hello, Doctor Giacchini? This is Detective Ralph Orloff of the Beverly Hills Police Department. I'm calling regarding a case I'm investigating. I would like to ask you a few questions about . . ."

"I know, Detective Orloff," Giacchini sharply cut in. "About the murder of Alfred Merrill, my dear esteemed colleague."

The adjectives Giacchini used were pronounced with such accentuation that Ralph felt certain that, for Giacchini, Alfred was neither dear nor esteemed. "And I suppose you wish to ask me what I was doing when Alfred was killed," Giacchini added in his Roman accent.

"Yes, well I . . ."

"I would be pleased to answer your questions, Detective Orloff. When can you be here?" Giacchini spoke as if in full control of himself and in total command of the situation.

Ralph heard the sarcasm that punctuated this offer. "This evening, if that would be convenient for you. I have some other interviews in your area this afternoon and will know more about the timing after six, if you'd like me to call before I come over."

"No need, I will be here all evening. Ciao," he ended in a marked staccato.

As Ralph placed the receiver back in its cradle, he could only hope Giacchini might be less curt behind the couch then he seemed on the telephone. After all, he wasn't counting on Giacchini to be more pleasant in person. But he hoped he was more amiable with his patients. Ralph realized, in that moment and to his amusement, that he was not only engaged in conducting a search for his analyst's murderer, but for his analyst's replacement as well.

CHAPTER 11

Show and Tell, Myths and Misanthropes

"Come in, Detective Orloff," Goldman said as he swung wide the front door of his home. He was a tall, slightly heavy-set man near Ralph's own age. He wore a plaid shirt, a string tie and faded blue jeans. His weathered complexion was framed by a carrot-colored, iron-jaw beard. Above an almost too-small nose twinkled cerulean eyes surrounded by dozens of what could only have been described as laugh-lines. A balding head, encircled by a fringe of shaggy, red hair topped off the picture of a man who seemed, if first impressions are worth anything, unable to keep secrets.

Ralph liked Goldman the minute he saw him.

As Ralph followed Goldman into what looked like the living room of the house, his wife, Sheila, a pert blond close in age to her husband, appeared from the kitchen with a dish towel still in her hands. Her hair, styled in a longish pixie-cut, hugged a face complemented by an abundance of freckles that were generously sprinkled over pleasantly pointy features.

Sheila Goldman had a tan like caramel coating poured over slim legs and arms that emerged out from under pink shorts, a white tee-shirt, and sandals. She seemed to radiate welcome without having to speak. They all sat in overstuffed gingham furniture in front of a tall tea-table, where a pitcher of lemonade and some freshly baked oatmeal cookies had been arranged on an antique Coca-Cola tray, accompanied by three glasses and some fan-folded gingham napkins.

"I trust I won't need to take up too much of your evening," Ralph said.

"Really no problem, Detective," Sheila said. "What can we do to help?"

"First, could each of you tell me where you were Friday between the hours of four-thirty and six-thirty?"

"Well," John pondered, stroking his beard thoughtfully. "I was with patients in my consulting room here in the house until ten to seven. That is, I saw patients on the hour until ten minutes to the hour most of the day. I had one at four, five and six. How about you, Honey?"

Sheila looked delighted, as if entertaining an old friend and talking about the glorious weather. "I was also in my office with patients until six-twenty."

"And where is that?"

"My office? Here at home, in the room out back. It used to be a garage, but we converted it to an office and a child's play-therapy room. You see, I also work with children." Sheila suddenly seemed to grow nervous. "Oh dear!" she said. "You won't have to disturb our patients in the course of this investigation, will you? I have one very disturbed little-one I see from four-thirty to five-twenty on Fridays, and I would hate to have the treatment complicated with some sort of police involvement."

"Hopefully that won't be necessary," Ralph said. "So, you were both here on the premises with patients?"

"Yes, that's right," the Goldmans answered in unison.

"Well, I wonder then how you might explain the appearance of that yellow 'fifty-eight Corvette that was seen in the parking lot of Doctor Merrill's office building around the same time of the murder." Ralph pointed out the window at the canary-yellow sports car in the driveway. "That *is* your car, isn't it?"

"Why yes, it belongs to us," John said. "But neither of us were driving it yesterday."

John rose and walked to the staircase. He called out to someone in the second-floor rooms above. "Honeybunch? Could you come down here a minute? There's someone I would like you to meet."

Within seconds, a young woman in her early twenties came skipping down the stairs and into the living room. She had long blond hair, the same color as her mother's, and the same bright blue eyes as her father. She was unmistakably a Goldman.

"Hi," she said to Ralph, holding out a dainty hand. "I'm Rachael."

"Sweetie, this is Detective Orloff from the police department. He wants to know about the 'Vet', where it was yesterday afternoon."

"Well, I had it, of course. You know that. I was at the Bio-med library at UCLA until about four or so and then I was at Doctor Ingersoll's office until close to six. After that I came back. She suddenly looked solemn. "Does this have something to do with Doctor Merrill's murder?"

"Yes dear, it does," her mother said. She turned to Ralph. "Does that answer your question, Mr. Orloff?"

"Yes, it does," Ralph said. "But I would like to ask Rachael a few more questions, if you don't mind."

"Sure. I don't mind," Rachael replied.

"When did you say you arrived at Doctor Ingersoll's office yesterday?"

"Oh right, I didn't say. It was a couple minutes past five. I didn't even get to sit down in the waiting room or anything. No time. Just flipped the switch and waited a sec, and she came right out to get me."

"And you left her office . . .?"

"At ten to six, of course. She always ends on time. If you can know anything about analysts, it's that they're always punctual,"

"Okay, did you happen to notice anything unusual when you were coming or going from Doctor Ingersoll's office?"

"Nothing. Except . . . hey wait a minute. There was a man getting into the elevator on the ground floor when I was leaving after my session" she said. "It was you."

"Yes, I was there," Ralph said. "And you're certain you saw no one else as you came into or left the building?"

"No. Well, except when I came in. I was in a rush, but I saw this really hot-looking woman at the pay phone downstairs. I noticed her just as the elevator door was closing. It was nothing, really. I only mention it because she was crying. I could hear through the closed door. I thought she looked familiar, but that's not strange. I mean, you always see the same people on the same days at the same times. So many people in analysis, I mean." Rachael paused for a moment as if thinking about something that was bothering her. "But I'd probably recognize her again if I saw her," she offered. "She was really gorgeous, with long dark wavy hair. She seemed so upset. I flashed on her image again when I came out of Doctor Ingersoll's office. I suppose because I was, well, sorta sad myself, in tears." Rachael's eyebrows went up. "You think that's important?"

"It could be," Ralph said, rising to leave. "I don't know yet."

Ralph thanked the family. John walked him to the door and wished him luck with the investigation. As he walked to his car, he reflected: A woman in tears, in the lobby of a building full of psychiatrists, was hardly unusual. The opposite—a woman laughing hysterically on the phone in that lobby—would have been more noteworthy. Still, it was worth keeping in mind.

He'd learned over the years that people have experiences that they push out of awareness, see things they dismiss as irrelevant, hear things they cast off as peripheral, and think things that seem irrational at the time. Ralph knew that all of these seemingly non-essential elements are stored in the unconscious, the seat of meaning; each perception will be offered up in a moment when it needs attending to. And in that moment, if one is able to bypass the censorship of so-called reason, one might learn from experience. Ralph's ability to cultivate this skill is what had made him a successful detective.

Bill and June Harrington appeared at the front door as Ralph walked up their driveway. Like the Goldmans, both were psycho-analysts, and both had known Alfred since his arrival in Los Angeles from London. They gave Ralph the impression that they were a couple who had grown, through many years of marriage, to look, behave, gesture and even to speak like each other.

"We were expecting you, Detective," two discomfited voices spoke as one. They invited him in.

Ralph stepped into a cozy if dated parlor. Its once-luxurious velvet upholstered furnishings were clean, although they conveyed a sense of use and stress from decades of wear. Theirs was one of those few homes in the flats of Beverly Hills that hadn't been 'mansionized.' It was as if its owners had, at least in their home, for decades resisted change.

"We've given thought to who among our people would do such a thing," June said. "We can't imagine what could have *provoked* such an attack on Alfred. Perhaps in a fit of narcissistic rage, a negative transference gone unattended to, perhaps a candidate. But even in a psychotic transference, we can't believe that Alfred wouldn't have seen it coming, that *he* would fail to take precautions,"

While June spoke for both with great agitation, her husband held and patted her hand, his brow creased with concern, frown lines deepening on the bridge of his nose, while nodding in agreement. Ralph learned during their conversation that Bill Harrington had been re-analyzed by Doctor Merrill. That is, he had been analyzed by Merrill years after the termination of his first analysis with another man during his training. The work with Merrill had ended some ten years earlier.

June Harrington had consulted with Merrill about several patients over the years. Both Harringtons thought very well of him; neither had a clue as to a suspect. Since neither one of them had their offices in the same building as their deceased colleague, they seemed to have nothing to report regarding the scene of the crime.

"We can only offer this," Bill said indignantly, as Ralph rose to leave. "It's difficult to imagine a situation in which any of us could have our throat cut while lying on our own couches. What I don't get is what possible conditions could prevail that would compel Alfred to lie down on his own couch while someone else was in the room? It's simply beyond imagination. If he were lying down when he was alone, let's say to take a nap, surely, he'd have been awakened if anyone entered the room. Even so, we all lock our doors when a patient is in the room and again when they leave. Besides that, he would've seen it coming. At the very least, he would've attempted to defend himself."

June agreed. "Exactly! My God, it's as though he was slaughtered like some sacrificial lamb on the altar of our profession."

Before Ralph could respond, Bill added, "There must be some sense, some meaning in this somewhere. You'd call it a motive, I suppose. Find that and you've found Alfred's killer."

"Look for a motive? Good idea," Ralph thought but didn't say. These people meant well. Instead, he held out his card. "Call me if you have any further thoughts." He gestured goodbye to the couple standing with their arms about one another.

Ralph drove off with a one-word summation of the Harringtons' ramblings perseverating in his own mind. *Revenge.* But whose revenge and for what transgression? Perhaps the nervous Doctor Dahlia Jacobs would provide some clues.

South of Olympic Boulevard, Roxbury Drive veers left past the grassy park, and intersects with those very same streets it previously paralleled. It was typical of the lack of city planning in Los Angeles, a city thrown together in a hurry and unaware that the population would grow so rapidly.

On the tree lined corner of South Bedford Drive, Ralph spotted Doctor Jacobs' address. It was one of those pseudo-chateau style condo buildings, painted in pale blue and topped off by a gray slate roof. He squeezed the big Buick between two Beemers and walked up to the double entrance doors. Dialing Jacobs' electronic security code, he heard, "Oh yes Detective, come up. I'm on the fourth floor. Apartment 404 just to the left of the elevator."

Ralph thought she sounded precarious, preoccupied. She'd sounded that way when he'd first called her. He wondered, as he waited for and rode up in the antique mirrored elevator, what made this lady so ill-at-ease.

"I hope you don't mind," came the voice from behind the closed door when he knocked. "But could you show me your badge or something? Just so I know it's you?"

"Yes, of course," Ralph said, flashing his identification a few inches from the peep-hole. Then he placed his own face within sight for confirmation. Almost immediately, he heard sounds of a chain being released and two dead-bolts being opened. A moment later, the door moved slowly. Barely widening bit by bit, the narrow opening revealing a lovely woman of around forty, with a fashionably full and pouty, pale pink mouth, eyes the color of dark roasted coffee beans, and wavy hair tinted burnt sienna. She wore a low-cut, silk caftan in shades of Indian summer and a pair of gold flip-flops on her sensuous, well-tended feet. This vampish visual version of Dahlia Jacobs was somehow incongruent with Ralph's auditory impression of an anxious, mousy mourner. Slowly she opened the door wide enough for the stranger to pass through.

"Please, come in," Dahlia said, in a more confident and inviting tone, now husky rather than hesitant.

"Doctor Jacobs?" It was Ralph's turn to ask for confirmation of identity.

"Yes. How can I help, Detective? Would you like a drink? I was just going to pour myself a glass of wine." Dahlia spoke over her shoulder, gesturing toward the sitting area as she made her way to the bar in the corner of the large, snow-white living room.

"Just some club soda, if you have it."

She poured from the two bottles simultaneously, with the expertise of a bartender, and joined him, seating herself at right angles to where he sat on the soft, sectional sofa.

"How long did you know Dr. Merrill?" he asked.

She drank nearly half her glass of wine before answering, as if she needed the fuel to give her answer. "I met Doctor Merrill—Alfred— when I was at the Reynolds-Durbin Child Study Center in 1980. He gave a paper on addressing envy and jealousy in the therapeutic process. I was so impressed, I attended all of his clinical seminars, and I had individual consultations with him as well. I suppose you'll find this out sooner or later, so I may as well tell you now. We were also lovers for a time."

"You were intimate with Doctor Merrill," Ralph said, thinking to himself *what good taste old Alfred had in women.*

"Yes, I was. But it ended nearly three years ago. I hated him then. But not anymore. I didn't kill him you know. But I think that I could easily have done so at one time."

Ralph nodded, deadpan. "Perhaps you could expand on that last remark, Doctor."

"You mean why could I have killed him, or when?"

"Both or either."

"Because he absolutely ruined my life, that's why," Dahlia snapped.

"And the when?"

"It was when I was taking his clinical seminar." Dahlia slipped off her sandals and put her feet up on the coffee table, sipping what remained of her wine. "Alfred had invited all of us, eight of us then, to his house for a barbecue. Lucienne—I assume you know she was his wife—was out of the country at the time. I stayed after the others had left, just to help him clean up. It was four years ago this summer.

I had just met Michael, Michael Pearlman. At that time, he was a young psychiatrist struggling with a somewhat latent aspiration to become an analyst. God knows why. We'd met at a party, dated a few times, had sex. I thought then that I was beginning to fall in love with him. He'd just begun his analysis with Alfred. Even though he, that is Michael, was four years younger than me, it didn't seem to matter much to either of us."

Dahlia stopped speaking long enough to have another swallow or two of her wine. "Anyway, it all came to an end that night. I'd had some champagne and wine, too much, but that doesn't really explain why I gave in to Alfred's seduction. It was really an irresistible set-up."

"Set-up?

"Yes. I'd always adored him, idolized him, really. He knew it. I fell for the oldest line in the book: *My wife doesn't love or understand me.*" Dahlia spoke as she stood up, walking to the bar to refill her glass. "Of course, the cliché was embellished by my own wishful fantasies," she continued, as she returned to her seat on the couch.

"Why clichéd?"

"The whole thing was so predictable. Alfred was old enough to be my father. How could I resist the overtures of a father who would choose *me* over his wife/my *mother*? Especially when my own father had taken off with my real mother, never to return to me again. They just abandoned me, left me with a maiden aunt, my mother's sister."

Dahlia took a deep breath and closed her eyes, their lashes so long that they rested on her high cheekbones. When at last she fluttered them open once again, Ralph noticed they were dewy, her eyes rimmed with red. "You see, my parents were both killed in an automobile accident while they were on holiday in Europe without me, when I was only eleven." She paused once again, apparently fighting back tears. "You know, I don't ever remember my father ever telling me that I was a pretty girl. But I do remember that night when Alfred did. And that night I felt, maybe for the first time, that I was the most gorgeous girl in the world. So, I became his. That is, until I realized that Lucienne was really the woman in his life.

"Guess I should have known she was the only one in his heart, too," Dahlia said, breaking down. "But by the time I got my wits about me, with the help of my own analysis, and realized that I was no longer eleven years old, Michael had grown tired of waiting for me to wise up."

As he witnessed Jacobs' defenses dissolve into tears, Ralph felt her hatred and her professional persona falling away, revealing a pitiable young girl, cast aside by a trusted elder. As Ralph allowed Dahlia's feelings of betrayal to grow inside himself as her surrogate, she appeared to recover her composure and went on to explain further. He pulled himself up short. Empathy was telling, but objectivity was necessary in the balance that makes a good detective.

"By the time I regained my sanity, Michael was seeing someone else—a captivating young diva from the LA Opera Company, the daughter of one of the other senior analysts in our society. It was only later that I learned that Michael had been influenced by Alfred to break it off with me, especially because he felt I was too old to give Michael children."

"Doctor Merrill told his own patient to break up with you?" Ralph attempted unsuccessfully to cover his amazement.

"Yes. He had actively discouraged Michael from pursuing our relationship out of his own possessiveness. Apparently, I was not alone in my feeling that I belonged to Alfred. It was clear to me at the time that he didn't want me, but he made sure that Michael wouldn't want me either. I felt bound to Alfred, but at the same time I also felt all alone and isolated. That's when I wanted to kill him."

"But you didn't," Ralph said.

"*No, I did not.* These several years in analysis have helped me to get over my hatred of Alfred, but it hasn't changed the fact that I'm forty-three years old and still unmarried."

Ralph thought how unfortunate it was that all the analysis in the world hadn't altered this woman's experience of being that little girl whose father didn't love her, one who had left her so uncertain of herself as a woman, that she was doomed to feel that no other man could or would want her, either.

After making a note to confirm Jacobs' statement that she had been attending a case conference at the mental health center until six on the day of the murder, Ralph excused himself and left for his meeting with Giancarlo Giacchini. He was somewhat surprised at himself as he noticed how eager he was to get away—to get away from Dahlia Jacobs, her story, and his own feelings of disillusionment with his former analyst.

Ralph replayed questions that had visited him earlier. *Was Alfred's murder an act of revenge? If so, whose revenge and for what offense?* Before driving off, Ralph made yet another note. *Look further into the connection between Merrill, Jacobs and Pearlman.*

Giancarlo Giacchini lived in one of those red-tile roofed and stucco villas on Peck Drive South. Old English roses and brightly colored Clematis crept in and out of the wrought-iron fence and up the walls lining the courtyard, where a small terra-cotta fountain sat singing a duet with a set of ceramic windchimes hanging in a nearby olive tree. Ralph knocked, but before he could step back from the heavy oaken door, a man who resembled a giant bear came up from behind him, seemingly out of nowhere.

"Detective Orloff, I presume? Let me introduce myself. I am Giancarlo Giacchini," he boomed, while extending a huge hand, covered in rawhide. Realizing at once that he'd forgotten to remove his gardening glove, Giacchini pulled it off apologetically. With a hearty chuckle he said, "*Scouse*, you will forgive me? I was working in the roses out back when I heard you drive up. So, I came around. I am sorry if I startle you. Won't you come in?"

Giacchini ushered Ralph through the front door, placed his pruning shears and gloves on the table in the foyer, leading the way through a wide arch down two steps into a spacious drawing room with furniture and artifacts straight out of a medieval Tuscan abbey. The pale, frescoed room was graced by a basket-woven tile floor, elaborate cornices, and coffered ceilings. Set before a splendid open hearth was a large and inviting sofa and several soft chairs, as well as a *Savonarola* that Giacchini had clearly reserved for himself with an open, leather-bound book resting on its seat. As they sat down, Ralph eyed the rose garden through the picture window, abundant with bloom-covered bushes displaying the fruits of what could only be the loving, personal attention of the master of the house.

"First, I regret having been so abrupt with you over the telephone earlier. You see, I was visiting with my daughter when you called, and she was about to leave." Giacchini added, with unexpected candor, "I would not be entirely candid if I did not add that any hostility toward Alfred Merrill, which you may have picked in my voice, is not an artifact of the timing of your call."

"I take it, then, that you were not friends."

"Allow me to say, we were never what you would call *close*. In fact, there had been much animosity growing between us throughout the years. Although I had respect for Alfred's dedication to the work, I am not what one would call a *true believer*. For Alfredo, this lack of fealty toward him on my part rendered any *friendship* between us out of the question in his mind."

"What was the nature of the friction between the two of you, if I may ask?"

"Is simple," Giacchini proclaimed. "Alfredo believed in the absolute power of psychoanalysis to make change, even to make cure in human physical ailments, not just mental. He emphasized the power of the word, both the patient's and the analyst's. He preached that there exists, merely waiting to be intuited and formulated by the analyst, of course, one and only one interpretation at any given point in the analysis. He was convinced that if the right interpretation were pronounced precisely, accurately, and in a timely manner, positive change must occur."

"I take it you don't agree with that notion."

"In my experience, there are things in life that cannot be analyzed away. Some things that cannot even be mitigated through analysis. In fact, there are dangerous traps one encounters in the analytic process. Traps for both analyst and analysand, should either one or both fall prey to the seduction of the ever-beckoning temptation to give in to an illusion of omnipotence. The danger lies in the mistaken belief that we can be the almighty *Zeus* to our patients."

"I'm not altogether ignorant of mythology, Doctor, but I'm not so sure I comprehend the analogy you're drawing between Doctor Merrill and the most powerful of the Greek gods."

"Yes, *Zeus of Olympus was* all powerful, omnipotent. Of him, *Achilles* said, *the eye of Zeus sees everything. His mind understands all.* So, tell me Detective, what else do *you* know of *Zeus*?"

Ralph played along. "Well, as I recall, he was the father of *Pallas Athena*, also known as *Minerva*."

"Bravo, Detective. Go on."

"He was said to have swallowed his wife, *Metis, the Goddess of Wisdom.* And if memory serves me, *Athena* was to be born, delivered at birth from the head of her father. I recall that *Minerva* is even depicted in ancient art as having sprung directly from the head of *Zeus*, fully armed, shielded, and ready for battle."

"Yes, very good, very good indeed. But there is also an unexplored *patricidal* element in this birth myth. For although there is an unusual bond between this father and his daughter, by rights of his having given life to her single-handedly, it was an ambivalent bond. You see, *Zeus*' head is said to have been split open in the process of Athena's birth. Also, there appears to be a *displacement* within the myth itself, a displacement of this patricidal element embedded in the act of decapitation of the *Medusa* by *Athena* or, depending on the version one subscribes to, by *Perseus* upon the order of *Athena*.

Freud himself equated this decapitation with the act of castration, which is perhaps why the warriors who gazed upon the head of the *Medusa,* either stuck on the end of the sword of *Perseus* or reflected on *Athena's* armored breastplate, were said to have been turned to stone. Perhaps they were actually frozen with fear at the sight of this most horrifying form."

"It also occurs to me that there must be some consequence of the absence of the mother in this story of *Athena,*" Ralph said.

"Detective Orloff," Giacchini laughed. "I am in awe. I never knew the police in this town were such learned men."

Ralph was also amused. He knew that he was allowing his unconscious to roam about, unfettered by the usual inhibitions of his profession. He was exploring his own mind, as well as the mind of his interviewer. Ralph knew, from a lifetime of experience, that this was a good sign. He always did his best work in this state of mind. "Perhaps not learned, but we do have our sources," Ralph said.

"Now," Giacchini said. "Let us get back to *Athena* and the absent *Metis*, who you will remember had been swallowed whole by *Zeus.*"

"And the consequences?"

"For *Athena* the consequences were grave indeed, I'm afraid," Giacchini said solemnly. "You see, she was the goddess of civilization, as it were. And so, in being cut off from her mother at birth, one might say that she was cut off from the basis of life, and from reason as well. She was as mind severed from body, civilization without Mother Nature's wisdom, out of touch with the earth and without common sense."

"Intellect without intuition," Ralph added.

"*Ecco!* Right on, as you say here."

"Of course, this is all very interesting," Ralph said. "But I feel at this moment as if I am cut off from the body of this investigation, with all this heady conversation about myth and psychoanalysis."

"*Chissa?* Only time will tell if our little talk proves to be of value to you or no. So, are there other questions you wish to ask of me?"

"Yes, there are other questions, but these are more on the order of the mundane, I'm afraid. For instance, what were you doing between four-thirty and six-thirty on the afternoon of the murder?"

"I was working, of course, in my office here in the back of the house. I have a group of therapists who consult with me weekly about their cases. They are here from five until six-thirty on Fridays. Before that, I see a patient from four until four-forty-five."

"You were with the group the entire time, of course?"

"Why, yes."

Ralph noticed a framed photograph sitting upon the heavy wooden mantle. He stood and moved to get a closer look. It was the photograph of a very glamorous, young, dark-haired woman. She looked vaguely familiar. "And if I need to verify your story, I can contact the members of this group, perhaps one or two."

Giacchini picked up on Ralph's agitation. "If it reassures you, I will gladly supply you with the names and the telephone numbers of all members of my group, Detective Orloff."

"That would be appreciated. Your daughter, Doctor Giacchini?" Ralph asked as he pointed to the photograph.

"Yes. She is my only child. Giuliana is her name."

"She looked familiar. For a moment, I thought I'd . . ."

"You may have seen her. You may even have heard her. Are you a patron of the opera here in Los Angeles?"

"With great strain on my budget, yes, I am."

"Giuliana used to sing with the opera."

"No kidding?"

"She was a soprano, a true coloratura. That is, before she lost her voice." Giacchini bowed his head, his mood noticeably fitting the alteration in topic. "It was a real tragedy. She was on her way to the pinnacle, such a talent, such an instrument she had. Then she began to have trouble with her voice just three years ago."

"That's too bad. What happened?"

"Her doctors finally diagnosed what they thought was an

operable laryngeal tumor. A very delicate surgery. They tried but could not save all her vocal capacities. She can speak, of course, but her singing voice, it is gone forever."

"Sorry to hear that." For a moment Ralph thought of his own daughters. "And what is your daughter's connection with Michael Pearlman?"

"Michael? We have known Michael for many years. He was a student of mine at the Neuro-Psychiatric Institute at UCLA when he was still a resident in psychiatry. And he and Giuliana, well I can tell you; they are in love. They were to have been married, in fact."

"Were?"

"That is, before the cancer. But since her surgery, she has not been herself. She has been embittered by her loss, and that has taken its toll on the romance. But it is my hope that they will find a way to overcome this heartbreak. After all, I look forward to grandchildren one day. Tell me, Detective Orloff, do you have children? Grandchildren?"

"Four children. And six grandchildren."

"You are a fortunate man."

Ralph left it at that.

CHAPTER 12

Untangling the Web

"Hey, Benny, my boy. Any news? What've you come up with so far?" Ralph inquired over the phone that night.

"Not a whole lot, but I'm beginning to get the impression these psychoanalysts are an odd bunch of bananas. Everything is very discrete until you scratch the surface. Then you find that Doctor A is supervising the work of Doctor B, who is in analysis with Doctor C, who is in supervision with Doctor D, who is the analyst of Doctor A. Get the picture?"

Ralph laughed. "I'm beginning to."

"I'm not joking here," Ben insisted. "It seems like one Freudian slip and confidentiality could go straight down the drain. Anyone fooling around in this group wouldn't have an ice-berg's chance in hell of keeping a secret for long. Eventually, word spreads from one couch to another, like lice in a kindergarten, and before you know it, the secret is pandemic."

"An open book, huh?"

"Book? A fucking tabloid. Boy, I'd sure like to be a fly on the wall in just one of these doctors' consulting rooms. If Merrill's murderer is somehow linked to this community, all I'd have to do is hang tight to find out who done it. On the other hand, when it comes to formality and respect for the privacy of the people *outside* the analytic family, I'm impressed with how tight-lipped and protective these folks can be. How 'bout yourself? You getting anywhere?"

"Well, I don't quite know what the connections mean yet. I'm finding a few loose ends myself. And I'm meeting with Doctor Ingersoll tomorrow to uncover some more information about Merrill's patients. I'm especially interested in the one that cancelled his appointment, originally scheduled for when Merrill was killed. Where will you be tomorrow? I'll give you a call when I'm finished with the Doc and we can meet, if you're not tied up with something else."

"Actually, I am tied up all day. My cousin is getting married, and I'll be in Laguna Beach for the wedding. Do you think you can get along without me? We'll talk first thing Monday."

"Sure, I got plenty to do. We'll see what we can piece together between the two of us next Monday. *Hasta la vista*, baby."

Ben did his own Arnold. "I'll be back." He hung up.

Ralph looked at the clock. Time to hit the sack. He set the clock for a relatively early wake-up the next morning.

He fell asleep so quickly, before he had a chance to dream, it was nine-thirty Sunday. Time to get going. He punched in ten digits.

"Doctor Ingersoll? This is Detective Orloff."

"Yes, Detective."

"I know we said that we'd meet at your office later today to discuss your contacts with Doctor Merrill's patients, but I haven't had any breakfast yet, and wondered if you'd care to join me for brunch. Unless, of course, you'd rather meet later in your office." Ralph hoped his invitation hadn't sounded as clumsy as it felt.

"Well, I am almost ready to leave my house. I have a few more calls to make, but I haven't eaten yet either and would enjoy your company. Where would you like to meet?"

"How about the deli on little Santa Monica? Do you know the one?"

"But of course, just around the corner from Bedford Drive. Could we make it in an hour and a half? I want to stop by my office first to make those calls. There are one or two patients I wasn't able to find yesterday."

"Of course. Then I'll see you at about eleven-thirty?"

"Until then," Claudine confirmed.

Ralph smiled to himself, forming a mental image of Claudine. Checking his watch again, he decided to see what Michael Pearlman was up to. From the listing in the Institute's directory, it appeared that he lived in one of those condos on Holmby Avenue off Little Santa Monica in Century City. There would be just enough time to stop off to interview him on the way to meet Claudine.

* * *

"Please, won't you come in," Pearlman said, as he shifted his eyes from the stranger who stood in his entryway toward the room on his right.

Ralph took the cue, went in and was immediately struck by the unexpected view of Century City that this otherwise unimpressive apartment had to offer. It was nothing less than spectacular, especially on one of those rare days when the air in LA is dry and clear and the atmosphere provides a stunning sapphire backdrop for the sky-scraping jewel-boxes that line the Avenue of the Stars.

"Great view!" Ralph exclaimed, as he turned back to the doctor. "Lived here long?"

"Two years, that's all. Won't you sit down? I'm having some coffee. May I offer you a cup? Cream or sugar?"

"Thanks, but I've had mine already."

Ralph took a seat in a wingback chair, sizing up the man who stood before him. Pearlman appeared to be a fellow in his late thirties, of average height and weight, with sable hair, a stalwart jaw, and dark, expressive eyes. Now they seemed to be conveying an urgency that gave Ralph the feeling that something was tightly wound up inside this man, just waiting to explode.

"Do the police have any idea who did this?" Pearlman blurted out.

"So far, we're still talking to people like yourself. People who knew Doctor Merrill. Could you tell me something about your relationship with him?"

"Why, I suppose, I just assumed you knew," Pearlman said, as he anxiously reached for the pack of cigarettes and lighter resting in an ashtray on the coffee table. "He was my training analyst." Pearlman lit up, took a deep drag, and continued. "I had a standing appointment with him Tuesdays through Fridays shortly after five, but this last Friday I had to be in Frisco to give a paper that evening. My flight left at four from LAX. I was picked up at the San Francisco airport around five-thirty by Tim Owens, an analyst from the San Francisco Society. We went to dinner before the meeting, which began at eight."

Growing visibly more restless as Ralph made notes, Pearlman said, "Detective Orloff, I understand from Doctor Giacchini that Alfred was probably murdered sometime during my hour. Is this true?"

"Yes, it is. The preliminary report from the coroner's office sets the time of death between five-thirty and six on Friday afternoon. I wonder if you could tell me who might have known that you had canceled your session on that day."

"Well, several people knew I would be flying out that afternoon. All the candidates in my class, many of the faculty members. But I'm not certain that I mentioned to anyone that I would be missing my analytic hour. Look here, Detective, surely you can't think that someone who knew me, who knew I saw Alfred at that time on Fridays, knew I'd be away during that hour, would go up there and kill him, just like that? That's absolutely insane."

"It may be," Ralph said. "I'm not sure Doctor Merrill's murder was the act of a sane person, whatever that means to you. It was almost certainly a pre-meditated, passionately motivated act, committed by a deranged person who knew him quite well. Now, who might have been aware that you were going out of town and would be missing your session that afternoon?"

"Just my fiancée, Giuliana Giacchini, and her father. Giulia was originally going to fly with me to San Francisco, and we were going to stay up there for the weekend. But our plans changed, and I flew up alone." Pearlman paused as he thought for a moment more. "Also, my control case supervisor, Doctor Collins, knew about my paper. I had to cancel my four-fifteen appointment with him as well. I think he knew that I saw my analyst after our meetings, since I was always in a rush to leave. He's right across the hall, you know."

"Uh huh. Anyone else?"

"Just Helen, Helen O'Connor, the Administrative Director of the Institute. She worked on the manuscript of the paper for me, and she knew I was going to present it that day. I might have mentioned having to miss my hour. I don't know, maybe not. Look, I think that's it."

"And what about your patients?"

"I don't see patients on Friday. I'm involved in a research project at the University that takes up most of the early part of my Fridays. In fact, the paper I was presenting in San Francisco was related to my research in psychosomatics."

Ralph came away from the interview with Pearlman with an uneasy feeling in his gut, as if something were gestating inside him, some new idea, something coming together just out of reach of his awareness. He drove on into Beverly Hills, parked in the metered lot behind the deli, and walked around the corner, just as Claudine was crossing the street. He waited for her to arrive at the curb, taking advantage of the time and the distance to contemplate her serene beauty. She was aristocratic, fluid in her movements, elegant, sleek, and sophisticated. She was so unlike his darling Dorothy, and yet Claudine, like Dorothy, radiated an aura of kindness.

"Hello. It seems we are in synch today," Claudine said almost coquettishly. "I'm starved."

As Ralph opened the door to the deli, he said, "Good. Me, too. And I have some things I'm eager to ask you about."

Ralph lost no time. As soon as they were seated and had ordered their brunch, he got down to it. "I've just learned that Michael Pearlman is *Michael_ canceled OT.*"

"Yes. I knew and I assumed that you would know by now. Have you spoken to him?"

"I just came from him, as a matter of fact."

"Then you know he was out of town."

"Yes. And that only a few people knew where he was going and when."

"Who else have you spoken to?"

"John and Sheila Goldman. And oh yes, Rachael Goldman, too." Ralph noted the glint of acknowledgement in Claudine's eyes. "Of course, that solved the case of the conspicuous Corvette as well as confirming your whereabouts, Doctor Ingersoll."

Claudine smiled, with just a hint of a blush.

"Then I spoke to the Harringtons, who gave me some food for thought about the relationship between the motive for and the method of the murder. After that I saw Dahlia Jacobs. A distressing story there. Then I had an interesting conversation with Giancarlo Giacchini about mythology. Or was it philosophy? Or maybe it was a lecture on the perils and pitfalls of psychoanalysis," Ralph said wryly. "I'm not sure which, but it seems he has a gorgeous daughter with a tragic story."

Claudine looked surprised. "You met Giuliana?"

"No. But I saw her photograph and heard about her fight with cancer, the loss of her singing voice. What a shame, huh?"

Claudine nodded silently.

"I also discovered that she's involved with our Doctor Pearlman," Ralph said. "Other than that, I can't say I'm any closer to finding

Alfred's killer than I was yesterday. So, I could sure use some help from you. That is, if you've learned anything from your contacts with his patients, anything that I should know about and, of course, anything that you feel you're at liberty to tell me about."

"I can tell you some things, but not all," Claudine said. "Apparently, most of Alfred's patients were candidates in training, just like Doctor Pearlman. Alfred also saw several candidates in supervision."

"So, what can you tell me?"

"I am certain you will meet these candidates in the course of your investigation. There are twelve individuals. I would rather not involve myself in these cases, if possible. However, if you do not uncover all twelve in your investigation, let me know and I will try to be of assistance. I really do not think you will have any difficulties with them, since they each expect to be hearing from the police and all wish to be cooperative. They may even come to you."

"And the others? The non-candidates?"

"Only two of Alfred's patients, eight hours of his practice per week, were individuals outside the Institute. Of these, one is relatively new, not even two years in treatment, very dedicated, suffering badly, no signs of negative transference, no signs of animosity toward Alfred. This person has requested a consultation with me, so we will be in contact. The other is a person of some celebrity. I do not see how this person could have murdered Alfred. You will have to rely on my word for this. Or else you must contact these people on your own." As though to punctuate her comment, Claudine took a sip of water. Then she added, "Of course, that says nothing about those patients who terminated their analysis in the past. Alfred's files are thick with old cases, you know."

"Nor does it rule out the possibility of someone new," Ralph added.

"That too is an option. I had not thought about it before, but he may have slipped someone, a new patient perhaps, into Michael's canceled hour at the last moment. Perhaps he forgot to mark this in his appointment book, although that is highly unlikely."

"Well, I've got a few more people to interview at the Institute and I'd like to get to those files and hear any speculations you might have. But for now, I want to ask you about something else."

They had to pause as their food arrived. Then Ralph proceeded to relate to Claudine as much as he could recall of his conversation with Giancarlo Giacchini, the myth of *Zeus* and *Minerva,* and the way in which he used it to make his point about the analytic work. When Ralph had finished, he noticed that Claudine looked troubled. "What are you thinking?" he asked.

"It occurs to me that Gianni may be referring to a debate that he and Alfred had on several occasions," she said. "A debate about the importance of the analyst's acknowledgement of external reality, whether in the patient's past or in his or her present-day life situation. Even in relationship to the analyst. Alfred was as convinced of his point of view as Gianni was of his own."

"That's hilarious," Ralph said. "I wouldn't think acknowledging external reality would be controversial."

She smiled without necessarily agreeing with him. "It's not quite that simple. Remember that what they argued about were *psychological symptoms.* The question was—the question *is*—are these symptoms caused by the body reacting to experience in the world? Or are they caused by the body reacting to the mind's reaction to experience? In the first, you treat the body. In the second, you treat the mind."

"And Alfred—"

"Alfred stood by his emphasis on *unconscious fantasy,* and his conviction, for example, that somatic symptoms are evidence of attacks being made upon envied and hated internal parental figures, and upon unwanted parts of oneself and one's experience. Gianni, on the other hand, was firm in his opinion that a somatic system or an organ could break down under the stress of continual use as a sort of bodily container for emotional experience that is just too disturbing to be thought about—too terrifying to be contained in the mind, as it were, and which might therefore be overlooked and left unattended to by the analyst."

"So," Ralph said. "Alfred thought that the body was attacking the mind's representations of bad parental figures or unwanted parts of the self. Giacchini thought that the body was wearing itself out, dealing with disturbing experiences. But you're talking about *psychosomatic* symptoms, right? Like a heart attack brought on by the stress of loss, or the growth of a cancer in someone who has recently lost a spouse?"

"Yes, something like that. Although, like Alfred, Gianni believed that such symptoms—however physically they manifested themselves—had a psychological component. They were a sign that the patient was suffering from some primary psychic experience, and that it needed to be received by and taken in, understood, and worked over in the mind of the analyst, and eventually by the patient in the course of the analysis. Gianni also stressed the importance of *non-interpretive interventions*. He would, on occasion, direct the patient toward seeking a medical evaluation and, if necessary, physical treatment for a symptom that he thought might have organic roots. Gianni was convinced that to address the somatic complaint by interpretation of the unconscious dynamics alone, was to risk colluding with the patient's demands for an omnipotent savior, as well as to invite a possibly lethal physiological catastrophe."

"I think I get it," Ralph said. "In fact, I'm remembering how, when I was in treatment with Alfred, I came in one day, preoccupied with my little daughter Judy's stomach cramps. The poor kid was in pain the night before, and it had kept me and Dorothy up all night. In the morning, I came to my session, but I worried about Judy. It was practically all I could talk about during the hour. Alfred kept bringing everything I said back to my childhood anxieties, which he insisted had been stirred up by Judy's pain. I was so pissed off at him. I mean, talk about external reality. It was as though he couldn't conceive of the fact that a father could be objectively worried about his daughter. I mean, sometimes a cigar is just a cigar, right?"

Smiling, Claudine tried speaking, but Ralph cut her off. "The problem was that everything that Alfred said was *plausible*. And I could feel that it could be true. But never once did he acknowledge the reality of my little girl's distress. Or that my distress could be objectively based on hers."

He sighed and sipped some coffee. "In fact," Ralph went on. "I was so distracted from my reality as a parent, that I didn't get around to calling my wife until noon. And guess what. I found out that she'd taken Judy to the emergency room with an acute case of appendicitis hours earlier."

"How dreadful!"

"I've often wondered what would have happened if I had come to Alfred complaining of my own stomach pains," Ralph said.

"And just what do you imagine?"

"I think I would've felt reassured that there was nothing physically wrong with me. And then, like any other macho cop, I would've stubbornly ignored the pain—that was clearly a symptom of *something*—and I would probably have ended up with a burst appendix and a bad case of peritonitis or maybe a bleeding ulcer." Ralph's eyes narrowed and his face muscles clenched.

Claudine nodded thoughtfully. "Yes, well then, you see Gianni's point. This was the essence of the running argument between Gianni and Alfred, at least in part."

They finished their meal in a hush until Ralph finally spoke.

"How well do you know Dahlia Jacobs."

"Quite well, actually. I was involved in her training. Why do you ask?"

"Because I thought you might know something about her involvement with Michael Pearlman."

"Only that they were together intimately for some time and then it seemed to end quite abruptly. Of course, she never really confided in me about it. But there were rumors that Alfred had something to do with the break-up. And around that same time it was apparent that Michael had become enamored of Gianni's daughter. As you probably know, they have been together ever since."

"You must be quite close with *Gianni*," Ralph said. There was an edge in his voice, as he emphasized Giacchini's name, pronouncing it *Johnny,* just as Claudine had.

"We are good friends." Claudine reached out across the table for Ralph's closed hand. "You are perturbed, Detective."

"Does it show? By the way, you could call me Ralph." He looked deep into her eyes, a grin spreading across his increasingly relaxed face, his hand opening to the touch of hers.

"No, Ralph, it does not show. How soon you forget, I'm psychic," she added playfully.

"Well, if you're so psychic, how about telling me who killed Alfred Merrill and why?"

"Let's go over to my office. I want to show you something."

At the Roxbury building they went into Merrill's office, where Claudine opened the metal filing cabinet. "These are the scant files Alfred kept on each of his patients," she said. "Patients he was seeing when he was killed, as well as those who had previously ended their treatment. It occurred to me that it could be someone who had terminated. Like yourself, for example," she added, her eyes sparking mischief.

"Ah, baloney." He feigned a sneer. "Ya got nothing on me, lady."

"Very persuasive. But seriously—you came back to see Alfred when you needed help, because you had a good experience with him in your analysis, one that you had been able to sustain since the end of your therapy."

"I'm sensing there's a 'but' to this."

"There could be others who may not have had such positive outcomes. Or perhaps there were those who were not able to maintain a benign mental and emotional connection with him after the actual physical separation."

"I'm not sure I get your point."

"Well, surely you must recall having experienced some disillusionment with your analysis—and with Alfred—after you ended treatment?"

Ralph reacted with surprise. "Yes, now that you mention it, I did. Even before this investigation. There were some things I'd hoped to accomplish—some changes I'd wanted to make in my life and in my relationships—that I was never quite able to pull off. That *was* disappointing. In fact, I think I was depressed for some time after the analysis ended. But mainly I was grateful to Alfred for all he did help me with. Analysis made an enormous difference in my life and especially my work."

"Did it?"

"Yes. In fact, I even went back and passed the bar exam a year after ending, just to prove to myself that I could do it—and even though I'd already decided against leaving the department to practice law."

"A lawyer, too? What a complicated man you are, Detective. So, even with such a positive outcome, you suffered from disappointment."

"Yeah, I did. I guess I missed our talks. I really missed him. But I got on well enough after a while."

"Then, you can imagine how you might have felt if the outcome had been unsatisfactory. What if you had left out of frustration? Or as a result of feeling betrayed and unfulfilled? Or, what if you had been secure and optimistic at termination, but slowly you noticed the gains of your analysis, little by little, dissolving into thin air as time passed, and you lost touch with the good experience?"

Ralph nodded. "That *would* be tough."

"And what if that gratitude gradually began to sour, finally turning into contempt or even hatred? You might feel cheated and humiliated. You couldn't tell anyone. Who would understand?"

Ralph thought of his colleagues, and of the stigma of being a cop in therapy. "Yeah, who?"

"It would be an indignity that you just might wish to conceal. Most people would think you crazy, in this day and age, just for submitting to such a treatment to begin with. After all, in the minds of most people, psychoanalysis is *passé,* is it not?"

"I think I'm getting the picture," Ralph said. "I'd feel ripped off. And that rage could just grow and grow, until . . ." He drew a finger across his throat.

"—until you felt you felt murderous?" Claudine said.

"So, our murderer might be in these files," Ralph agreed, pulling out his own file and leafing through it.

"You know, of course, that these files are in no way complete records of any treatment," Claudine warned. "Like so many of us, Alfred only kept certain types of notes."

"Meaning—?"

"For example, if a patient is in a suicidal state of mind or is experiencing some kind of physical symptoms, one would ordinarily document such things for justification of treatment."

"For an insurance company? Or maybe to protect oneself in case of some possible future legal action?"

"No, not really. People who have been formally trained as psychoanalysts are more or less well-screened for sociopathy and other extremes of psychopathology before they begin training, and the analysis one undergoes in training usually helps one to maintain sufficient self-awareness to keep certain restraints and boundaries in place. So we're less likely to face such suits. For instance, we are not generally known to have sex with our patients or supervisees, or to inappropriately interfere with their lives and the lives of their loved ones. We also refrain from giving advice. Hopefully we learn to respect the potential in every patient to live his or her life independently. That is, when given the proper support and space to think about their predicaments. And another point, we rarely prescribe drugs of any sort."

"Not even the psychiatrists who are analysts?"

"Well, even the psychiatrists among us usually will not administer medication to their own analytic patients."

"Why not?"

"Because it can complicate matters. You see, we want the patient to realize that we are interested in his thoughts and feelings, no matter how disturbing these are to him. At first, he may only wish to get rid of his more uncomfortable emotions and ideas. Of course, we do not attempt to impede him, if that is what he needs to do. But neither do we want to be seen as surreptitiously colluding with his desire to evade handling painful life experiences. Medications fail to get to the root of the symptoms, and may only get rid of them temporarily, often with many deleterious side effects over time. In analysis we endeavor to engage the patient in an exploration of the source of his symptoms, whether they be depression, anxiety, or even hallucinations. That's how we uncover meaning."

"And once the meaning is exposed?"

"We hope that it may provide a shield that the patient can use to protect himself against the symptoms. For example, against the threat of terror or despair in each new situation that resonates with painful experiences of childhood. We trust that this process might—with time, of course—allow for the patient's realization of his own capacity to think, to make meaning of what has happened to him."

"A Herculean task," Ralph said. "No wonder analysis takes so many years."

"Yes. So, to get back to Alfred's files, there may be notes on individual hours with a given patient. As I think you may know, Alfred wrote papers for publication, for scientific presentation and discussion with other analysts. He would have made notes for these purposes as well. Such notes might be verbatim re-constructions of certain sessions, or perhaps dreams occurring at crucial junctures in the treatment. These would have been jotted down only after the hour, and therefore must be considered only as representative of the therapeutic interaction that had occurred."

"They'd really just be notes based on the *analyst's version* of what occurred in the session."

"Yes. And it is also important to keep in mind that these would be expressive of very selective moments in an analysis. They may be significant only as they pertain to a given theoretical construct. And since these are only small slices of the clinical picture taken out of context, it is hard to say of what value they will be to your investigation."

"In short, we don't know what we'll find," Ralph said. "And you're concerned that we could err with regard to any inference we might make based on such sketchy material." Ralph felt it was his turn to reassure Claudine. He touched her hand. "You know, if you were to go over these files with me, I might be less likely foul things up. Believe me, Claudine, I don't wish to disturb a single hair on the head of any one of Alfred's patients, past or present, if I can avoid it. But there is a killer out there, and I have a job to do."

She brightened. Apparently, she didn't need much convincing. "Then let's get to it."

CHAPTER 13

Envy, Hurt and Jealousy

Ralph dreamed that night.

He's watching a film or a play, close-up, sitting in the front row of a theatre. The Latin words 'Vexet Minerva' are engraved on a shield carried by a Roman soldier who swoops down from the sky, wings waving, his sword held high over his helmeted head. Just as the winged soldier touches down on the ground, he beheads a giant bear crossing his path.

But as the bear falls, the soldier's own helmet falls off, revealing a head full of long, dark curls. Only then can Ralph see that the soldier is not a 'he' after all, but a young woman dressed as a man. She is talking to someone on the phone when she suddenly falls to the ground, clutching herself and crying

"My tummy, Daddy it hurts, please help me!"

Her voice finally fades away, and all that Ralph can hear anymore is a faint echo as he wakes up with a start.

"It's Monday morning. And we're gonna start out this fine summer's day with the sound of David Benoit and his trio . . . on K-JAZZ . . ."

Ralph reached over and shut off the clock radio next to his head. He reached for his phone and hit a saved number.

Ben Hollinger answered. He sounded stressed. "Yeah?"

"Dude. This is your wakeup call."

"I don't remember asking for one."

"We anticipate your every need. Wanna get an early start?"

"Sure, man. Why not."

"Touchy, touchy? Rough night, cowboy?"

"I wish. Breakfast first?"

"Let's meet at Merrill's office. We can go over what we've got so far."

"Okay, I'm game," Ben said. "Give me half an hour. Oh, and bring some coffee, will you?"

"Your wish is my request." Ralph hung up. He thought about his dream as he pulled down the metal thermos from the shelf over the counter in the kitchen and started brewing the coffee.

It seems too straightforward to be straightforward.

The dream was like a collage of visual metaphors, various elements of several conversations he'd had over the weekend: one with Giacchini about *Athena-Minerva*, one with Claudine about his daughter, Judy, and the brief exchange with Goldman's daughter, in which she'd mentioned a young woman with dark curls.

Rachael Goldman had seen a woman in the phone booth in the Roxbury building. The woman had seemed familiar to her . . .

Suddenly the ringing telephone interrupted Ralph's train of thought. He answered.

"Ralph? This is Claudine. Are you coming to my office today?"

"As a matter of fact, I'm headed over there right now. Why?"

"The memorial and funeral for Alfred will be tomorrow afternoon, and I thought perhaps we could go over the remainder of the files in case it might help you. I mean, to identify and to observe anyone who might be at the service or the grave site. You will be going to the funeral?"

"Yes, of course I'll be there. I was also thinking of paying a visit to Helen O'Connor. She's one of the few people who may have known that Merrill would be alone in his consulting room between five and six."

"That is a good idea. If you can get her to talk with you, she could be an invaluable source of information. She knows everyone in the Society. Almost all the faculty and students have confided in her, at one time or another. She is like the 'house mother' to us all, candidates and teachers alike. She's a central hub for personal and professional complaints. She's a keen observer too."

"Sounds like a key player. Then again, she might be like a mother-hen protecting her chicks from any nosey fox poking his snout into the coop."

Claudine laughed. "Yes, that may be true."

"I'm wondering if I might not get more out of Ms. O'Connor if I had you along with me when I pay her a visit."

"You may be right. If you would like we could go together after we see about those patient files."

"Thanks. That'd be a big help. Look, I'm meeting my partner Ben in less than half an hour. I'll see you there. Or I could drop by your place and pick you up, if you like?"

"I would like that. I'll wait for you out front."

Ralph made a note of Claudine's address on Selby Avenue in Westwood. Then he dialed the number for the Institute. The machine answered. "We are either out of the office or on another call right now, so please leave your name and number. . ." Ralph hung up.

On second thought, he decided, it might be most advantageous for the fox to make a sneak attack on the coop. After filling his oversized thermos with steamed milk and coffee, he pulled his jacket off the hanger in the front hall closet, scratched Custer behind the ears one last time, and locked the door behind himself.

As Ralph drove Wilshire Boulevard East to Selby, he attempted to re-visit the dream. He pondered the decapitated bear and, besides the obvious, was reminded of Giancarlo Giacchini. His first impression had been that Giacchini himself was ursine—a very large and imposing man, with thick, unkempt eyebrows, a full dark heavy beard, hairy arms, a furry chest that protruded from his shirt, and a head of black hair that had not seen a barber's chair for many moons.

Hair.

Long hair.

Long dark curls.

In the photo he'd glimpsed in the Giacchini home, Giuliana had hair like the woman in his dream. Two other items in the dream stood out:

The voice that faded into an *echo* at the end of the dream, and the motto *'Vexet Minerva'* that appeared in the beginning. He wondered why he had recalled these two bumps in reverse order.

Or was he over analyzing?

Maybe. But maybe. . . .

Just as Ralph pulled up into the driveway of her house, he could see Claudine locking the front door. Turning toward the car, she greeted Ralph with such an engaging smile that all but thoughts of her became irrelevant. It was wonderful and revivifying and he hoped it didn't last forever. He did need to concentrate on the case.

When they arrived, Ben was already in the hallway, waiting.

"Well, I'm pleased and honored you two decided to join me." He reached for Ralph's thermos. "I could really use some of that."

Ralph jerked it back and said, "And you are—?"

Ben grimaced. "Sorry." He smiled at Claudine. "Nice to see you again, Doctor Ingersoll," he said

Claudine unlocked the door, stepped inside and turned on the lights. Ralph poured some coffee into the cap of the thermos and handed it to his partner, and said, "So, what have we?"

"Well, I've been through everyone on the list, from Andrews to Freedman, and the only one so far that gets me excited is this Doctor Collins. He gives me the creeps, if you really want to know."

"Oh no, not Daniel," Claudine said. "He's a pussycat."

"Lions are pussycats, too," Ben said. "And they've been known to kill an animal or two."

"But we've already spoken to him," Ralph said. "I thought I'd crossed him off your list. How'd you get to him?"

Ben pulled a notepad from his inner pocket and flipped it open. "I had an interesting conversation with a certain Doctor Karen Fowlkes. It seems she is quite a fan of our Doctor Collins. Had supervision with him for years before coming to the Institute for training. When she matriculated, she started her didactic analysis with Merrill, mainly because she admired Collins so much and knew he'd been analyzed by Merrill, too." He stopped and looked earnestly at Ralph. "You didn't bring any, like, muffins or anything, did you?"

"Sorry. It wasn't on the order."

"Whatever. Anyway . . . it turned out that there was quite a surprise waiting for Fowlkes when she hit Merrill's couch. She told me that Merrill tried to tear her down, right from the start of the treatment."

"What do you mean, tear her down?" Ralph asked.

"Fowlkes said that Merrill verbally hacked away at her, trying to undercut her self-esteem. Merrill let her know, in no uncertain terms, that she didn't know shit from Shinola when it came to psychoanalysis. She said it sure seemed more like brain washing than therapy. It didn't take long for her to get over her admiration of the good Doctor, and she left him after a few short months."

"Quit her training analysis?"

"Yeah, quit cold turkey."

"Can you do that?" Ralph asked Claudine. She nodded.

"Guess so," Ben said. "At least she did it. She said it was tough going, at first. It seems that the graybeards of the Education Committee of the Institute look askance at a candidate who wants out of their analysis early on in the treatment. But she was persistent, so they granted permission for the change."

"Then what?" Ralph asked.

Ben looked over at Claudine, who had remained sphinxlike throughout the telling of his story. "Well, it seems she's quite satisfied with her work with you, Doctor Ingersoll."

Claudine nodded modestly.

"Anyway, to make a long story even longer, Fowlkes mentioned in passing some incident that had taken place at a scientific meeting, not long ago. I think she said it was in June, when our Doctor Collins gave a paper expanding upon Merrill's work."

"An incident!" Ralph said. "Incidents are interesting."

"Ya think? Anyway, it seems Merrill was supposed to formally discuss Collins' paper at that meeting. But when the time came for his discussion to begin, he got up and admitted that he had not read the paper prior to the meeting, which I'm told is just not done in this polite society. Disrespectful."

"And . . .?"

"Then he proceeded to talk about his own work, ignoring Collins' paper completely until the end. Fowlkes told me that Merrill had suggested, with a patronizing tone, that there was nothing new or timely about Collins' paper, but that its value—if any—lay in its simplistic reiteration of what Merrill had put forward over twenty years before."

"Whoa. That's cold."

"Yeah. Pretty provocative. And Fowlkes, who's sitting with Collins during the whole time, told me that Collins looked—" He flipped the page in his notebook and read a quote. "— 'absolutely livid.' And, uh, she said he muttered under his breath something about cutting the throat of that ball-busting son-of-a-bitch someday." Ben shrugged. "Okay, but which of us *hasn't* ever said something like that? Apart from the three of us and everybody we've ever known." He put the notebook back in his pocket. "Anyway, there you have it. Respectfully submitted, et cetera. Any idea what it means?"

"It means nothing," Claudine said. "Everyone says intemperate things."

"Maybe," Ralph said. "It's worth asking why Fowlkes told you in the first place. In any case, we'll get back to it. Let's get to the files."

The three began to plow through some thirty manila folders in the file drawer marked *inactive*. The majority of the terminated cases were training cases, candidates in the institute. They were all persons who had either been or who were about to be interviewed. Around mid-afternoon, Ralph and Claudine left Ben looking for anything in the files that required follow-up, while they drove over to West Los Angeles to talk with Helen O'Connor.

Helen addressed them as they came through the door to the administrative offices of the Institute, a friendly expression on her face that seemed to fit her earth-mother appearance. She wore flowing ethnic garb, sandals, and a collection of beaded necklaces that dated back to the sixties. Although she must have been close to sixty, she wore her hair in a loose braid down her back, and bracelets encircled both arms nearly half-way to her elbows.

O'Connor's eyes were the color of dark brown sugar, with little laugh lines generously scattered outward from the corners that accentuated their shape and size. She was definitely built for comfort, quite tall, with a fulsome, feminine figure and that kind of dark auburn coloring of both hair and complexion found only in a true Irish *Cailin*.

"Well, hello, Doctor Ingersoll," she said. "I thought I might be hearin' from you."

"This is Detective Ralph Orloff from the Beverly Hills Police, Helen," Claudine said. "Mr. Orloff is investigating Doctor Merrill's murder and I have been assisting him as best I can. And how about you? How are you getting along?"

"Well, as you would expect. The phones have kept me busy. Everyone is very upset and well, as you can imagine . . . bewildered." She seemed about to go on, but suddenly stopped.

Claudine noticed. "Helen, Detective Orloff really needs our cooperation. So, I think it would be best if you spoke as candidly as possible about anything that might even remotely pertain to Alfred's death. Now, you were about to say something else."

"Well, as I was saying, everyone is upset." Helen's eyes shifted to and fro, between Claudine and Ralph. "The worst of it is Mrs. Merrill, of course. Oh, and Doctor Collins. They've both been after me to help contact everyone about the funeral. It's at two o'clock tomorrow, but I suppose you know. At Westwood Cemetery. Those two are a couple of basket cases, if you ask me. Poor Kurt is trying his best to keep them from falling apart, but he could use some help himself, so if you could just look in on the three of them, Doctor Ingersoll."

"Yes, of course. I will do that. Is there anything else?"

"Well, then there are Doctor Merrill's candidates."

"Yes. They're taking it quite hard, aren't they?"

"Hard? That's an understatement. Lily Bergin is hysterical. She says it's because she was in the midst of a negative transference when she left him on Friday morning. Poor thing, she's only first year, and this was her very first summer holiday break. She said she slammed the door after telling Doctor Merrill that she hoped his plane would crash. Then she said that she slammed the door and could hear elements of the ceiling falling to the floor. She really acts like the whole thing is her fault, poor baby. As guilty as she's feeling, I'm surprised she hasn't been over to see you by now to turn herself in.

"Then there's Paula Freedman. She's second year. Said she hadn't been able to talk that whole last hour with him. Said she'd wanted to tell him she loved him and that she needed him, something like that. She wanted to plead with him not to go, but she said she just couldn't risk letting him know how much he meant to her." Helen paused, then directed her comment to Ralph more than to Claudine. "I don't know how these adults, each of them with more degrees than you can shake a stick at, can lose all perspective in a prone position. I know it's that transference thing. They do, too. But the feelings are powerfully strong."

"Yes, that is true," Claudine said.

"I swear, no ordinary person would believe it. If you didn't know these people in other situations and in other capacities, you'd have the whole bunch certified and shipped straight off to the funny farm."

"It is remarkable, the transformations that take place on the couch."

Ralph thought about some of his own more humbling if not downright embarrassing regressive episodes. He flashed back to one moment when he was sure that Merrill was a tiger, about to spring at him from behind. Ralph was compelled to prop himself up on one arm and had turned to find his analyst with his hands folded in his lap, a thoughtful and kindly look in his eyes, all attentive to what his patient had been speaking about.

"Oh, and I also had a visit from Randall Hart today. He's fourth year and more than a little bit in denial if you ask me."

"What makes you say that?"

"Well, he said that he had already looked into who was still in town this summer to get some appointments lined up. He was eager to start another training analysis. Said he had a difficult control case in the works or some such thing and needed the support. Didn't even want to wait 'til fall to make the arrangements. Can you imagine? Why, poor Alfred's body isn't even in the ground, and *that one* is interviewing his replacement."

Helen was outraged. Ralph seized the moment to ask the crucial question.

"And who had left town before Friday, Ms. O'Connor?"

"Well, no one actually. No one left before Friday. No one I know of left on Friday or afterward, for that matter. Except Michael Pearlman, who went to San Francisco late Friday afternoon to give a paper at a conference or something. And you and the Merrills were supposed to leave Friday night," Helen addressed herself to Claudine. "I think most of the others, those who were scheduled to leave town on Saturday or Sunday, canceled or postponed their holidays when they heard the news Friday night on TV, or certainly by Saturday morning when it hit the papers."

"Has everyone been notified of the funeral?" Claudine asked.

"Yes. I think I've emailed all and I've spoken to or left messages as well for just about everyone." She looked at Ralph. "Detective Orloff, are you thinking it could be someone in our Society? I mean the murderer?"

"Are you, Helen?" Ralph returned the question.

"Well, no. But Sylvia Sidwell was in here today, and you know how she is, Claudine. She's such a troublemaker. You always have to take what she says with a pound of salt."

"Yes, you do," Claudine said.

"Sometimes I can even get close to feeling sorry for her. I know she simply can't stand being left out of anything, so she always acts like she has the inside story. I've certainly fallen into that trap more than once. Spilling the beans, thinking that she knew it all anyhow, only to find out later that she didn't know anything at all. And neither did she have any right to."

"I've had such experiences with Sylvia, too."

"It appears that Sylvia can hardly bear it when two people have a relationship, unless she can insert herself in between them, like a baby nestled between her parents in their bed at night," Helen went on. "But look out, because if she can't snuggle in between, she'll wedge herself in forcefully. She'll do it with a crowbar, breaking up everything on either side in the process. If you ask me, and I'm no analyst, sometimes it seems that Sylvia intends, for better or for worse, to destroy other peoples' lives when they're not solely dedicated to her."

"I do know what you mean, Helen," Claudine agreed.

"I guess that's why, when she came in today, it was no surprise that she was just spreading her poison about as usual."

Ralph's interest increased. "Poison?"

"Oh, I don't mean that literally. She just says things. Like, *it sure is fortunate for Lucienne Merrill that she has Kurt Cross around. It's so nice to have a man around the house,* she crooned at me, and she was off key, I might add, as she sashayed all about the office. Then she said, *sure wouldn't mind having those big broad shoulders to cry on, would you?* I mean really, can you believe the nerve?"

"Unfortunately, I can," Claudine sighed. "Absolutely. Yes. Anything else, Helen?"

"Well then, if that weren't enough, she asked if Daniel Collins would be giving the eulogy at the funeral. She said that she thought it would be appropriate for *Oedipus* to say a few nice words about *Laius,* before bedding down his mother, even though *Laius* had left him wounded and all alone to die in the wilderness. By Oedipus I supposed she meant Doctor Collins, and of course, even I could see the reference to Doctor and Mrs. Merrill. Have you ever?"

By this point, Helen was worked up and on a tear. "For all the world, it sounded like she wanted to provoke me to be suspicious of Doctor Collins, of all people. As if he could kill for power in the Institute. And then, before I finally told her that I had work to do and insisted that she leave, she suggested that Alfred might have had a lover who might have been so jealous that she would be moved to murder. She made sure to remind me that Doctor Jacobs, Doctor Mills and Doctor Pincus had each had *a thing* for Doctor Merrill at one time or another, and that you, Doctor Ingersoll, had been very lonely since your husband's death, and now to lose Alfred as well. She just couldn't contemplate how bereft you must be. Especially since *it had happened while you were right there in the suite the whole time.* Why, the nerve of that woman! She just makes me so mad."

"Helen, you know Sylvia," Claudine said, trying to soothe. "I am surprised that you would let her get you so worked up."

"I know, it's silly that she can get to me, after all these years.

But sometimes I think she could make me doubt my own mother," Helen chuckled.

"She sounds like a very unhappy woman, this Doctor Sidwell," Ralph said, "Did she know Doctor Merrill well?"

"Did she ever. Why, she used to be his vassal, but something happened and the chill that set in between those two over the years made the cold war between America and the Soviets seem like a neighborhood marshmallow roast." Helen added, "Of course, the back-biting was usually discretely confined to gatherings of the members of each one's own personal clique. But just about everyone knew that there was no love lost between those two."

"And how was that?"

"Well, some thought it was because Sylvia was a psychologist and a literary type as well, not a medical doctor. A *feminazi* they called her, and a closet *Lacanian*. And himself, being delivered straight out of the bastion of the Harley Street Kleinians and a male chauvinist to boot, well it only seemed to follow . . ."

"Please," Ralph said. "Could you translate? I'm lost somewhere between the Lacanian closet and 'Harley Street.'"

"Oh," Claudine said. "What this must sound like to a lay person and an outsider. It is probably not of the tiniest importance, but Lacan was a French psychoanalyst who was very charismatic and so he had many ardent followers. They were known as Lacanians. Lacan believed that the unconscious, at least that aspect of the unconscious that is accessible to us through the analytic process, is structured in much the same way as is language."

Ralph gestured: And—?

"For example," she went on. "A language is made up of signs and signifiers, words that may have either a precise or an evocative meaning, as well as a certain order and cadence that is necessary for the maintenance of that meaning. Disrupt the order or the tempo, and the meaning is altered or obliterated altogether. For Lacan, this alteration or obliteration of meaning in the unconscious was the basis of neurosis, and even psychosis. He firmly believed that language provides the singular means of deciphering the unconscious and of restoring the natural order of the mind."

"I'll buy it," Ralph said. "Or at least rent it for a little while."

"But Lacan was quite a controversial figure in French psycho-analytic circles, especially since he did not adhere to the classical Freudian framework of the fifty- or even the forty-five-minute hour. Instead, he thought that the analyst must end the hour when the pinnacle of emotional involvement is reached in the session, even if that peak occurs five minutes into the session. He thought that for the unconscious to remain open, the session must be terminated at the point of maximal contact, rather than being allowed more time to seal over again before ending."

"Doesn't sound very satisfying," Ralph said.

"Precisely as it's meant to be. There was literally no closure." Claudine continued, "Lacan insisted that this lack of satisfaction could aid in disabusing the patient of his infantile belief in the analyst as the sole possessor of knowledge and love. For Lacan, this was the goal of the analysis. The key to the resolution of the transference neurosis was to know and love thyself."

"So, a *closet Lacanian* is someone who practices the Lacanian technique of analysis, but doesn't advertise the fact?"

"Correct."

"And Harley Street?"

"Harley Street is in London. It's very well-known as the place where only the cream of the medical profession practice, including some of the most successful psychoanalysts. The street has a reputation for exclusivity—for a certain attitude if you wish."

"And, if you ask me," Helen interjected. "Alfred's attitude contributed to the whole problem of *closeting* of all kinds. And not just with Sylvia Sidwell, but with many of our faculty and students. People were downright deflated by him at times. His exclusivity was deadening."

"You're saying he was intimidating," Ralph said.

"Yes," Claudine sighed. "I'm afraid intimidation is a good word for what Alfred sometimes practiced. Many of my colleagues often felt that they would come under public criticism—and, in fact, they *did* come under public attack from Alfred and his followers, when their ideas strayed from the party line."

Helen added, "Many folks kept their ideas to themselves on account of his attitude. Believe me, I know. I heard about it when they were upset and had no one else they could talk to."

Ralph decided to voice what all three of them were probably thinking. "So, this is just great. Suppression of ideas . . . repression of feelings . . . fear of expressing yourself . . . and in a group like this."

Claudine nodded. "It is ironic."

"It is ironic on stilts," Ralph said. "But that's not the worst of it. The question is, could the frustration related to this kind of censorship move an otherwise sane individual to commit an insane act?" He smiled at Helen. "Call me when you've figured it out."

She winked. "You'll be the first to know."

After leaving Helen, Ralph and Claudine returned to Beverly Hills, where they had arranged to meet with Ben at C.A.P.S. headquarters. Upstairs, they found him sitting in his cubbyhole, his chair swiveled to take advantage of the view northward up Rexford Drive, an impressive street, lined on both sides with mansions, fronted by carpets of manicured greenery.

"Daydreaming?" Ralph said.

"Thinking," Ben replied as he swung around.

"Same thing, in my book." Ralph pulled over a third chair for Claudine and sat down in his own at the cubicle across from his partner's. "So, what do you have to show for all your hard work?"

"I've interviewed the A's though the F's and each has an alibi that checks out. Just what you'd expect. Either they were with patients or with supervisees. But going through those termination files in Merrill's office, I ran into something curious. You interviewed

Giancarlo Giacchini, didn't you?" Off Ralph's nod he asked, "Is he related to Giuliana Giacchini?"

"She's his daughter. Why?"

"Because I think she must have been a patient of Merrill's."

"You think?"

"Well, there's a file with her name on it."

"Huh. Funny. Giacchini didn't mention it when we met. So?"

"So, it's empty."

"The file is empty?"

"It's the only one that is. No, wait, it did contain one thing. A pressed rose."

"A what? Rose?"

"Yeah, a rose. The flower. You know that thing which by any other name would smell as sweet."

"You mean there's nothing in the file about treatment or termination? Just . . . a rose," Ralph was incredulous. "Weird."

"Especially since all the other files have notes and copies of insurance bills, correspondence from the patients, and record of calendar dates—starting, ending, birthdays, that kind of stuff. But not for this Giacchini chick. Just a dried, pressed rose. Like a corsage a girl might save from her big night at the prom."

The two men turned to Claudine in hopes of receiving some clarity. She looked back with an unreadably neutral lack of expression. Ralph recognized it as her *closed-for-reasons-of-patient-confidentiality* look.

"I suppose we will need to have a talk with Ms. Giacchini about this," Ralph said. "Don't you think so, Doctor?"

"That would seem prudent," Claudine said.

Ralph sighed. "So, find anything else, cowboy?"

"Well, there were some notes in a few of the files. Mostly descriptions of dreams. The ones that get me hot and bothered are the ones that depict murder."

"Interesting."

"I'll say. And—"

"Although," Ralph added. "It wouldn't surprise me if the ones that did depict murder were the dreams of people who couldn't possibly actually commit murder in real life."

"I wouldn't know," Ben said. "Anyway, it sure makes for peculiar reading. I thought that maybe the Doc here could have a look at them and give us an idea if there's something we should pursue, or if it's just symbolic stuff."

"Could you do that for us, Claudine?" Ralph asked.

"Yes, I will review them. But remember, I may not be able to tell you anything conclusive. As long as you understand, I am willing to try."

"Fantastic," Ralph said. "You two head over to the office and do some dream analysis, while I drop in on Giuliana Giacchini and her rose garden."

CHAPTER 14

Ben and Jerry

As Ben and Claudine walked up Roxbury from the parking lot, Ben saw a familiar figure, a man on the corner with a big black boom box resting on his shoulder, pressed against one ear. Rain or shine, offshore winds or onshore gloom, Jerry could always be seen hanging out somewhere in that golden triangle of medical and professional offices and expensive boutiques bounded by Little Santa Monica Boulevard to the North, Wilshire Boulevard to the South, and Crescent Drive to the East.

Jerry was almost always decked out in his uniform: a black, hooded sweatshirt, matching sweatpants, and black, high-topped Nikes. Today he was doing his Michael Jackson moonwalk on the sidewalk, looking as if he didn't have a care in the world.

"There he is," Ben said. "Jivin' Jerry."

"I've seen him around here often," Claudine said. "Is that what the police call him?"

"Yeah, a living testament to our humane and civilized public mental health-care system."

"He is doing well, compared to most," Claudine said.

"The restaurants around the triangle keep him pretty well fed, actually. And just the other day I saw him in Hills' Electronics. Seems his boom box was on the fritz, so he brought it in. The owner took it in, fixed it up, and sent Jerry merrily on his way, as content as a kid at Christmas. He was mov'n his feet to the beat, like always."

"Yes, he does have a number of people who look after him," Claudine said. "As a matter of fact, one of our analysts monitors his medications. He told me that Jerry shares a place with a few other victims of President Reagan's institutional reform. They live in a halfway house with no medical supervision."

Ben abruptly stopped in his tracks, his face set in a deep scowl.

"What is it?" Claudine said.

"You know, it just occurs to me that our man Jerry there is quite the creature of habit. It's four-thirty now, and he's almost always here at this time. Then, around six-thirty, he moves over to Bedford or Camden, hangin' in the alleyway behind the restaurant kitchens, looking for a gourmet hand-out."

"Do you mean . . .?"

"Could be. He might have seen something last Friday. Something or someone out of the ordinary. Well, we'll soon find out."

Ben marched off briskly in the direction of the dancing man, with Claudine close behind him. "Jerry, my man!" Ben shouted. He reached out as he approached to offer a high-five.

"I didn't do nothin', man, I swear it," Jerry pleaded in a terrified tone as he recoiled from the approaching policeman, lifting his free arm above his head as a gesture of submission.

"That's what they all say," Ben chided as he grabbed Jerry's raised arm, pulling it down and around, turning him toward the wall of the building. He spoke in a steady, low voice. "Co-o-o-o-o-l it, man! Don't panic just yet. I just want to ask you a few questions. O.K.?"

Jerry wiggled free from Ben's grip and turning to face him. "Yeah, man, but don't hurt me. Okay?"

"Right. Now suppose you tell me where you were last Friday about this time of day."

"Hell, man," Jerry pleaded. "I was right here on this street, man. You know that. You see'd me here before. This is my job, man. My place. My corner. I entertain here 'til six-thirty and then I take up my post in the alley behind *The Grill*. Then after the dinner hour, I go right home. Home by ten, by curfew with the lights out, just like my momma always said."

"Yes, you're a good boy, Jerry. And that's why I know I can rely on you." Ben put his arm around the other man's shoulder. "You see, I know that *you* know nearly everyone around these parts. So, I thought you would notice if there were anyone around here that didn't fit in. You know, someone new, maybe?"

"No, man," Jerry said, shaking his head. "I can't recollect anyone last Friday. Anyone new, that is. But wait a minute. 'Bout what time did you say?"

"Between four-thirty and six-thirty."

"No one new. Not that I recollect, anyway. But I did see someone I ain't see'd in a lo-o-ong time."

"And who might that be, Jerry?"

"Well, I don't rightly know her name, of course. We ain't been formally introduced, you see. But weee-oooh! She's one fine and lovely lady, that one. She used to come 'round here I'd say maybe five days a week for three, four years. But then, long about two years ago, she was no mo'. That is, not until last Friday on my watch."

"And what did this good-looker look like?" Ben coaxed.

Jerry was suddenly as if unleashed. He went off in a singsong, clanging, rhythmic rhyme that was his customary style, accompanied by a jaunty dance step. "Oh man. What'd she look like? Like a million bucks, a Valentino tux, like one of them Black Glamma mink coats, like a chocolate ice-cream float, a Tiffany diamond, a song by Paul Simon, like a—"

"Okay, okay. I get it. She was *fine*. But what did she *look like*? Hair, eyes, figure, clothes . . . real stuff. . I'm a simple, uneducated guy, Jerry. Not a poet like you. So dumb it down for me."

"No problem, Mr. *Po-lice-man*. She about so tall," Jerry said, holding his hand up midway on Ben's chest. "She had long, dark hair, all wavy and curly-cue down her back like so," Jerry gestured with both hands below his shoulders. "And the smoothest skin pulled jest right up over a most *vo-lup-tu-ous* frame, with T 'n A that could straighten out half of West Hollywood, if you know what I mean." He laughed. "Can't recall the wrapper, but I sure do remember what was inside the package. That is, when I unwrapped it in my mind. Weee-ooo! And, oh, one more thing."

"What's that?"

"She went into 'dat building right over there, jest like old times."

Jerry pointed to the same building Ben and Claudine were about to enter.

Merrill's building.

"And in case you're about to ask, yes sir. I could pick her out of a crowd on Rodeo Drive during the Christmas rush. A real dazzler. Not too likely to forget a bird like that, even after she done flew the coop."

Ben was tempted to ask Jerry what exactly that last phrase meant—how had the young woman flown the coop? —but thought better of it. With a witness like this, you took what you could get. He thanked Jerry for his help, then ushered Claudine into the building.

They were in Merrill's office going over case folders, with a special search warrant from the court, when Ben noticed a shiny black Jaguar pull up in front of the building onto the street as he glanced out of the window. A dark-haired man in his late thirties, looking quite fit if a little stiff, emerged from the driver's seat of the car. He sported a black, three-piece suit and carried a gym bag. After placing a handicapped placard in the windshield, he looked both ways, up and down the street, before locking the door of the car door.

Ben couldn't help but notice that the man walked quickly into the building without bothering to put so much as a dime in the meter. Ben was annoyed. He imagined that this relatively young man was abusing the system. But maybe he was being too harsh. After all, this *was* a medical building. It could be the man was picking someone up from an appointment with a doctor, an elderly mother perhaps, or a disabled spouse.

"That's Randall Hart," Claudine said. She had come up behind Ben and had seen Hart's arrival. "He'll have a file here." She opened a vertical file drawer, flipped a few files forward until she reached H, and extracted one, which she gave to Ben.

Ben read it with interest. Randall Hart's file was filled with notes on dreams with repetitive violent themes. One was of particular interest to the detective. The doctor's notes were simple to make out.

Hart is on surgical rotation at County. The nurse wheels a man into the OR on a gurney. He is bleeding and the blanket covering him is soaked with his blood. Hart pulls back the wet blanket and sees that the man's penis has been mutilated. Hart begins suturing at once, but his patient is criticizing his every move. 'You idiot!' the patient yells at him. But Hart continues working.

However, the man won't shut up. He's making Hart so nervous he's afraid he will botch the job. Hart tries to explain to the patient that he must stop shouting at him, but he continues to go on and on. Hart puts out his hand to the scrub nurse on his left and calls for a scalpel. She slaps one into his hand and Hart makes a deep incision into the man's neck, severing his vocal cords. Then Hart returns to his work, suturing the man's penis, until the nurse says, 'It's no use, Doctor. He's gone'.

Other dreams noted in the file involved rivalry with other men for women, with other patients, for positions of power in the Institute, and the murder of the father who ridicules him for his ineptitude.

A note made only one week before read, *"Must consider this patient unsuitable at present for analytic work. Can no longer overlook virulent streak of psychopathy as yet unmodified by any interpretations made. He shows absolutely no remorse for his blatant attacks upon his objects. His arrogance continues unabated to date. Consider taking this up in Progression Committee annual Fall review."*

"This one's a charmer," Ben said.

Claudine seemed to have waited for Ben's reaction. She nodded. "He's more than a bit anti-social, but murder? Well, I have serious doubts about that."

"What do *you* mean by anti-social?"

"Well, I can recall when I was chairing the committee on Continuing Professional Education, there were several complaints from candidates who helped out monitoring the registration at scientific meetings. Randall nearly always attempted to slip in without paying an admission fee. And once, when he was participating in a series of lectures presented by various candidates for the general mental health community, he clipped out the section of the advertisement for the program that announced his own lecture, pinned it up on bulletin boards in all the various graduate school and university campuses, while excluding the notices for any of the other speakers."

"A prince of a guy," Ben summarized.

"He is also known to be terribly imperious with the other candidates, even with some of the senior faculty. He has little if any regard for his colleagues. Rumor has it that he recently married for money and prestige. I hate to say it, but he manipulates almost everyone. In fact, I've even heard a rumor that he has somehow acquired a handicapped parking permit for his car—under false pretenses, of course—and has been said to park in handicapped zones and at parking meters, without putting money in the meters."

"I think that I can confirm that rumor." Ben thumbed toward the window. "Is that Jag his?"

Claudine glanced out the window at Hart's car and sighed. "Yes. It was a wedding present from his wife." She added, "Of course, some would say these are small things. But taken as a whole, the pattern is quite disconcerting and demonstrates a significant lack of integrity, unbefitting someone in our profession."

"Don't students ordinarily get expelled or suspended for that kind of behavior in professional schools?"

"To tell the truth, some of the faculty—including myself—had attempted to have him dismissed from the Institute. But Alfred always comes . . ." She paused. ". . . always *came* to his rescue. That is until recently."

"How recently?" Ben turned once again to the window and the Jaguar below.

"A few days ago, Alfred was fussing and fuming, angrily moving about the office before our first patients arrived for the morning. It was last Monday morning. He had taken in Saturday's mail before I arrived, and when I came in, he was cursing under his breath."

"Pissed off?"

Nodding, Claudine continued. "I couldn't help noticing, as he handed me my mail, that he was holding a notice from his bank with a check attached. I asked what was so perturbing, he was slamming doors and drawers and it was obvious to me that he needed to get something off his chest."

"What was that?"

"He told me, in an uncustomary breach of confidence, that Randall had bounced his monthly check for his analytic sessions for the third time this year. Alfred even finally admitted that Randall was hopelessly unanalyzable. He said that he was on the verge of agreeing to Randall's dismissal from the training at the next meeting of the Progression Committee, no matter how bad it made him look."

"And did he?"

"He never had the opportunity. The next meeting is scheduled in September, after the holiday break, just before the start of the Fall term."

"No kidding . . ."

"Maybe we'll just have to have a little talk with Doctor Hart." Ben looked pensive for a moment, then added, "You know, I could have said, we'll have a little heart-to-heart with him. But I didn't."

Claudine nodded with great solemnity. "You are most kind."

CHAPTER 15

Roses and Thorns

Ralph pulled his Buick up in front of the Giacchini home. The garage, now open, revealed two cars: an older Mercedes and a green Fiat sport with the top down. As he approached the garage, he heard an engine accelerate and tires squeal. He was very nearly run down by the small car, as it lurched backward out of its stall, screeching to a sudden stop just shy of Ralph's knees.

"Oh dear!" From the driver's seat, Giuliana turned toward Ralph, her curls bouncing. "Are you alright? I'm so sorry, but I didn't see you."

Ralph offered his I.D. "A miss is as good as a mile, Ms. Giacchini. I'm Detective Orloff, Beverly Hills Police. I met your father on Saturday and thought maybe we could talk for a minute or two? That is, if you can spare the time. If you're not in too much of a hurry."

"Not at all, Detective," Giuliana said shyly, eyes downcast in embarrassment and shame. "I always drive like this. But I'm sure you're not here to give me a ticket for reckless driving," she applied the handbrake and cut the engine. "Actually, I was just going out for a drive to the beach. To meet someone. But I have time. Would you like to come in for a while? My father is inside but we can talk there."

"Thanks." Ralph wondered who, if anyone, she planned to meet at the beach. "I'll try not to take up too much of your time."

He opened the door and helped the young woman out of the car. They walked together through the courtyard. Just as Giuliana put her key in the door, it opened unexpectedly revealing the velvet-robed figure of her father.

"*Buon Giorno*, Detective Orloff. And what brings you here this day? Giuliana, *cara mia*. I see you two have already met. Well, come in, come in, won't you?" Giacchini swung the door wide open and stepped aside to allow their entrance.

"I was hoping to have a few words with your daughter, Doctor Giacchini," Ralph said.

"With Giuliana? Well, if you wish it, I am certain she will cooperate fully, won't you, cara?"

"Of course, Papa. We can sit in the living room, if that's alright, Detective?" Giuliana said.

Without waiting for a response from either, Giuliana turned and walked into the sitting room, where Ralph had first spoken to her father. Settling herself in one corner of the couch, feet tucked up underneath the full skirt of her sundress, she looked younger than her years. Her father seated himself protectively by her side on the couch. Ralph took the opportunity to try out the *Savonarola*.

"I realize such things are usually kept very private," Ralph said. "But I know you'll understand that I need to know something about your relationship with Doctor Merrill."

Giuliana coyly smiled. "Yes. Well. I thought you would be by sooner or later."

Expressing his obvious bewilderment, Giancarlo stuttered. "Detective Orloff? Giulia? What? I am afraid I do not understand."

"You must excuse my father, Detective."

"Giulia!"

"He wasn't aware of my analysis with Doctor Merrill."

"*Madonna mia*," Giacchini yelped.

His daughter reached over for his hand before she continued. "You see, Papa didn't approve of Doctor Merrill. Or, shall we say, his methods."

Giacchini was stunned by his daughter's revelation. "Giuliana Lucia Rosanna Giacchini, but how could you?"

"It was really quite easy, Papa. After all, you weren't given to prying into my comings and goings."

"But if I had known . . ."

"Weren't you the one who taught me that one's analysis is a very private thing?"

"But Merrill? Of all the. . . . You knew I would never . . ."

"Which is perhaps why I chose him, Papa. Precisely because I knew you would never have approved of him for me."

As if to assuage his wrath, she snuggled up to the older man at her side, kissing him on his furry cheek, reminding Ralph of such moments with his own daughters. Ralph felt sympathy for Giacchini as he recalled how Karen and Judy used to wind him around their little fingers, without so much as a smidgen of guilt or shame. Was there a daughter in the world who didn't own her father's heart from the moment of her birth?

Giancarlo crossed his arms over his chest, biting his lip.

"Now papa, don't take it so hard," Giuliana said, stroking his chin.

His arms dropped down, and his lips relaxed into a smile as he looked into her exquisite face.

"Wasn't that a predictably adolescent thing for a daughter to do? Some kind of denial of my adoration for you, Father," she asked. "To choose a man who is nothing like you, a man who was the antithesis of you, Papa." She turned to Ralph. "Anyway, it didn't last too long, as you must know. I left his couch two years ago. Against medical advice, I might add."

"As far as I am concerned, the more you do against Alfred Merrill's medical advice, may his soul rest in peace, the better," Giancarlo snarled.

"You see, Detective Orloff, rebellion runs in the family."

"So, I take it that you haven't seen Doctor Merrill since you terminated your analysis," Ralph said.

"No, I haven't. Is that all you wanted to know?"

"Actually, there was one other thing. A single dried, pressed rose was found in your file. Or rather, in the records Doctor Merrill kept in a file with your name on it. Can you tell me anything about it?"

"A rose? In my file? I have no idea what you're referring to." She reached for a cigarette from the *cloisonné* box on the table in front of her. Then she paused for a moment before lighting it. "Not unless. . . . Wait a minute. There was one local performance of mine that Doctor Merrill attended. It was my performance as Violetta in Puccini's *La Traviata*. I remember seeing him, sitting in the front row." She moved the lit match to the tip of her cigarette and inhaled deeply. "During the third curtain call, someone handed me an enormous bouquet of violet-colored roses, *Blue Nile* I believe they were. I removed one bud from the bunch and threw it to him. Just for the drama of it, of course." She smiled. "He actually brought this up in the next session. Alfred never had any sense of romance. Funny, I'd forgotten about it until now."

"If he had no sense of romance, you'd have to wonder why he kept it," Ralph said. He stood. "Too bad we can't ask him. Anyway, thank you, Miss Giacchini."

As Ralph headed toward the exit, Giancarlo stepped in and led the way. Then, at the door, Ralph stopped suddenly and turned back toward the room. "Oh, just one more thing. "May I ask where you were between four-thirty and six-thirty last Friday afternoon, Ms. Giacchini?"

"Why, I was . . . let me try to recall. I was here, I believe. Yes here, here at home. I was resting in my room all afternoon."

"Anyone who'd be able to corroborate that?"

"Not really. Our housekeeper takes off for the weekend at about three on Fridays and Father works until after six," she said. She seemed to avoid eye contact with her father.

"I see," Ralph said. "I also understand you decided not to accompany Doctor Pearlman to San Francisco that day. Why was that?"

"I felt tired. I haven't been well lately, and I just decided not to make the trip with him this time. That's really all there is to it, Detective."

"Of course. Very sorry to have taken up so much of your time." Ralph turned again toward the door, still held open by the Doctor. On crossing the threshold, Ralph turned toward him, snapping his fingers. "Oh yes! Excuse me Doctor. Just one more thing." He strode back into the living room, where he found the young woman now gazing out onto the rose garden. "Pardon me, Miss, I was wondering about just one more thing."

Giuliana looked at him without mirth. "Is this your Columbo act, Detective?"

"Is it that obvious?"

"Yes, it is. But go ahead. What else can I tell you?"

"Could you say why you interrupted your analysis with Doctor Merrill, against his advice?"

She spoke flatly. "Yes, I'll tell you why I ended my analysis with Dr. Merrill. Because he didn't *get* me, Detective Orloff. It's as simple and as complicated as that. Alfred Merrill simply didn't see *me* at all. He never understood."

"Meaning—?"

"He completely underestimated me."

CHAPTER 16

Memorial Montage

Turning into the alley passing alongside the AVCO Cinema multiplex off Wilshire Boulevard, Ralph and Ben followed the drive that circled around the very exclusive, if small, private cemetery. Most Angelinos wouldn't even know of its existence, it's so hidden from the public eye.

The names of those interred in the Westwood Village Memorial Park Cemetery include movie stars and other famous figures, like Eve Arden, John Boles, Fanny Brice, Truman Capote, John, Cassavetes, Oscar Levant, Marilyn Monroe, Mario Caste Nuovo-Tedesco, Francis Len Taylor, Natalie Wood, and Darryl Zanuck. The detectives parked behind the growing line of mostly expensive late model cars and walked to the chapel where the memorial service for Alfred Merrill was soon to begin.

"This guy Hart never returned your call, huh," Ben said.

"Not yet. I was wondering about him, too, ever since Helen O'Connor told us that he was already out hunting for a new training analyst. Could just be one callous, self-absorbed, thoughtless parasite."

"In L.A.? Surely, you jest."

"Or maybe his sociopathy is more extensive than anyone had thought possible," Ralph said.

They attempted to blend in with the throng of mourners entering the vestibule of the chapel. Inside Helen O'Connor and another woman were greeting people as they came in and stopped to sign the mourner's registry.

"Hello, Detective Orloff," Helen said in a businesslike tone. "This is Doctor Melissa Mills. She's one of our candidates. Doctor Mills, this is Detective Orloff and . . .?"

"Detective Ben Hollinger," Ben said.

"Detective Orloff and Detective Hollinger are with the Beverly Hills Police, investigating Doctor Merrill's death," Helen said to Melissa.

Melissa Mills was an enchanting woman, with long, curvy eyelashes, long silky hair, and long legs. She was dressed all in black, from her cashmere turtleneck sheath, down past black stockings to a neat pair of ebony kid-skin pumps. She was otherwise adorned only by a single opera-length string of unspoiled white pearls.

"You were a student of Doctor Merrill's?" Ralph inquired.

"A supervisee, yes," Melissa said. "It's shocking. Do you have any idea yet who the murderer might have been?"

"We're still in the preliminary stages of the investigation. But we're making every effort to follow-up on any and all leads at this time, Doctor Mills."

At that moment, a familiar voice softly cried out. "Detective Orloff!"

Ralph heard Claudine and turned, just as she emerged from the crowd.

"I would like a moment with you, if I may?" Claudine said. "Will you excuse us, Melissa, Helen?"

Claudine took Ralph's arm, steering him to one side of the entrance. When they were clear of the others, she confided in a discrete whisper. "Forgive me if I have interrupted anything important, but I have heard something quite troubling just this morning."

"No problem. What's up?"

"On my way over, I stopped at the office. I had left my appointment book on my desk and wanted it with me, should one of my patients call and fail to leave a number. I was getting out of my car, when that homeless schizophrenic man, you may know him as *Jiving Jerry,* I believe, approached me and told me that he had read about Alfred's murder in the newspapers. He had apparently recognized his photograph. He said that he had something to tell the police. Detective Hollinger spoke with him yesterday, you know. Nevertheless, he asked me if I could arrange for him to speak to the senior detective on the case. He said that he would meet you on Roxbury at five this afternoon."

"Did he give you any hint what it was about?"

"He said he could identify Alfred's lover."

"His lover. Did he say anything else?".

"No. Just that he could identify her."

"What did you tell him?"

"I only told him that I would contact you. I said I was certain that you would be in touch with him."

"That's fine, Claudine, just fine. You did exactly the right thing."

"Did Ben have the chance to tell you about his talk with Jerry yesterday?"

"Yes, he did. Maybe Jerry remembered something else. Or maybe he hallucinated something else. I suppose we'll just have to wait and see. Meanwhile, I have a question for you. Who's this Doctor Mills? Do you know her well?"

"Oh, yes," Claudine said She looked relieved to change the subject. "She's just one of our post-seminar candidates. That is, she has completed the seminars, but is still in supervision on her clinical cases. She was one of Alfred's supervisees. I haven't had much contact with her, with the exception of one class that I taught, and which she attended in the very beginning of her training."

Ralph nodded. Then he asked, "Is Mrs. Merrill here yet?"

"Yes, Lucienne is inside with Kurt. As a matter of fact, I was just going into the chapel to sit with her. Poor thing. She has really grown more and more raw these last few days. I think she could use my support, and I believe they will be starting within minutes anyway. It is nearly two. Will you be joining us?"

"No. I think we'll have a better view of things from here. Will I see you later?"

"There will be a reception at Lucienne's home after the service at the burial site. I am sure we will see each other there."

"I'll be there. Oh, by the way, is Randall Hart here?"

"Why yes. See? Right over there with Dahlia Jacobs." Claudine's gesture directed Ralph's attention toward the right side of the isle, in the front row inside the chapel.

"Thanks," Ralph said, crossing the room in Ben's direction.

The younger detective was deeply engaged in conversation with an older analyst. The man was extremely tall and thin, with dark shaggy hair, badly in need of shampoo. He bore a marked resemblance to Abraham Lincoln.

"Ralph," Ben said. "This is Doctor Mathias Donaldson. He's the current Dean of the Institute. Doctor, this is my partner, Detective Ralph Orloff."

Donaldson nodded politely. "Mr. Orloff. I was just telling Mr. Hollinger here about Alfred's ground-breaking work, improving the outcome of our therapeutic encounters with what we call the psychotic aspect of the personality."

"Psychosis?" Ralph questioned. "I wasn't aware that you could treat psychotics."

"Some think psychosis is treatable. Others don't. But what I'm referring to is the analysis of the *psychotic part* of the personality, which can be detected in many patients who do not warrant the psychiatric diagnosis of psychosis. We come up against this aspect of the mind, even in our garden-variety neurotic patients."

Ben looked intrigued. He gestured toward Donaldson and said, "Check this out."

"You see," Donaldson went on. "Often times, let's say with the kind of murderers you might run into in your work, one kills or attempts to kill someone they know intimately. Perhaps a lover, a spouse or relative. We believe that these people invariably have isolated out, from their conscious awareness, many years of grievances and the emotions connected with such grievances. Now, this may not apply to someone like say, Anthony Sorrentino, a serial killer. I do recall hearing you were active in that case, Detective Orloff. But it would apply to, say, someone who commits what the police might refer to as a crime of passion."

"You say these grievances are isolated in the unconscious," Ralph said.

"Yes, they are defensively cordoned-off from consciousness very early on in childhood. And when they are encapsulated in this way, these aspects of experience take on a life of their own. In isolation, they are not afforded a chance to be modified by beneficial experiences later in life, but instead they fester and grow like a cancer."

"An anti-social element?" Ralph asked.

"Not quite. Not anti-social but more *asocial*, for lack of socialization while in an encapsulated state," Donaldson replied, in his soft-spoken way. "In other words, they're *without reason*. They form their own code of conduct outside the realm of shared social reality. They exist without benefit of rational social interaction. They are deprived and become out-laws.

"This is the very essence of what we call *the psychotic aspect* of the personality. The seed or core. And this aspect of the personality seduces and beguiles the more healthy and adult aspects of the character, coaxing them into going along. However, when seduction alone fails to control a situation, the psychotic part of the personality takes over by use of coercion and force. It literally overwhelms the remainder of the personality, which is usually weakened due to a lack of healthy aggressivity and assertiveness since, in its isolated state, it has been deprived of contact with these healthy mitigating aspects that have been commandeered by and which act in service of the psychotic part of the personality."

"Wait up a minute, Doctor." Ralph held up a finger as though for a point of information. "Let me make sure that I understand what you're saying. To me, this psychotic or criminal part of the personality sounds something like an incarcerated felon. You know some sociologists argue that in prison, the criminal is not rehabilitated, but instead becomes a more proficient criminal. Maybe you're suggesting that this isn't just because they are surrounded by other criminal types, but due to isolation from any positive influences."

"Exactly," Donaldson concurred. "And, like a criminal who is turned loose in society, this felonious aspect of the personality can hold that *society of the mind* hostage and may wreak havoc if it's not held in check. One moment of personal madness, not unlike a prison break, sets the killer free. And before the ego or the agent of pro-social sanity has the opportunity to apprehend and regain control over the criminal aspect of the mind, that outlaw can do irreparable damage."

"And afterward?"

"Afterward? If you mean, after the damage is done, perhaps in some cases overwhelming guilt and despair set in, often suicide or . . ." Donaldson paused.

"Doctor?"

"Or the use of denial or any number of other psychic defenses set up against the overwhelming impingement of such guilt feelings—defenses that can even lead to increased criminality, I'm afraid."

Ralph realized that Donaldson had been on a manic roll, headed downhill fast. But mourning was inevitable after a period of intellectual defense. Ralph could recognize this pattern, even while he too was trying to keep his head above the waves of depression if possible by engaging in this kind of academic banter.

"But eventually, these defenses become like sandbags positioned to shore up a dam under threat of collapsing in the wake of an ever-rising tide of mud and water. Eventually they give way, and the torrents of guilt, like the waters on a flood-plain, inundate the personality, and depression often leads to suicide or suicidal behavior, or more likely sub-intentional efforts to be found out."

"What do you mean by sub-intentional?" Ben asked.

"Perhaps the killer might be inclined to leave clues to insure being caught and persecuted by *extra-psychic* agencies, such as the police. Quite a welcome relief from the *internal persecution* that can take place, eventually driving one to suicide," Donaldson said. "In short, Detective Orloff, I believe you will catch up with Alfred's murderer. Dead or alive, he or she will be discovered. Mark my words."

From your lips to God's ear, thought Ralph. "I like your theory and hope it proves valid, Doctor."

Nodding, Donaldson excused himself. "I'm afraid I must take my place inside now. We'll begin soon. I'm delivering the eulogy. As you may have known, or perhaps may have guessed, Alfred was once my own analyst."

"It's a small world, isn't it, Doctor?" Ralph muttered almost inaudibly as Donaldson turned away.

"So?" Ben said. "Hot stuff, huh? What'aya think?"

"I think that what our Doctor Donaldson had to tell us was no *obiter dictum*. He's pointing a finger alright, but it's not clear yet at whom," Ralph said, as he carefully scanned the chapel. "Looks like they're starting, let's take a seat."

Ben and Ralph sat down in the last row as Doctor Donaldson took the podium. He carried a small black book, which he laid open in front of him. He thanked all for coming. Ben took notes of each name mentioned.

Donaldson continued with a short prayer in Hebrew.

Ralph's eyes wandered to the front row, where Claudine sat next to Lucienne Merrill. Kurt Cross flanked her left side, wearing a three-piece charcoal suit and looking not at all like the cowboy he'd met earlier. Next to Kurt sat Melissa Mills, with Dan Collins and another woman who appeared to be his wife next to him on the aisle. He was hunched over in his seat and the woman's arm was draped on the back of his chair.

Ralph listened as Donaldson cleared his raspy throat, and all grew silent in preparation for the eulogy.

"Alfred Merrill was many things to many people. He was a husband to Lucienne, a father to Kurt, a friend and colleague to his peers, and an inspiration to candidates. To his patients, he was a healer, just as he himself had once been healed. As a lover of truth, he saw analysis as a vehicle for the truth, and the analyst as the driver of that vehicle. Indeed, he drove the truth home to us all with his wit, his charm, and his never-ending confidence in analysis, in his own analyst, and all those psychoanalytic forefathers. He was unflappable to the end when, without a struggle but with dignity, he must have faced the ultimate envious attack on his capacity to communicate the truth, and. . . ."

Ralph listened to Donaldson's eulogy while continuing his scan around the chapel, making a mental inventory of body language, faces and expressions, in reaction to the words spoken to honor the deceased. He noticed along one row, a group of younger people, mostly women. Among them were Paula Pincus, Lily Bergin, two women mentioned in Merrill's notes but seemingly distant. There were also Dahlia Jacobs, Randall Hart, Michael Pearlman and of course next to him, Giuliana Giacchini.

Ralph recognized the elder Giacchini sitting in the next row, behind his daughter. Beside him was a woman who fit the description of Sylvia Sidwell. What an unlikely pair they made, Ralph thought. Doctor Giacchini with his dignified European good looks, resembled a gruff but gracefully aging film idol. A king-sized Marcello Mastroianni came to mind. In contrast, Sidwell, with gaunt, wrinkled, and angular features topping off a small bent frame, was garbed in a drab and shapeless gray suit to match her steel-colored hair, severely pulled back in a bun at the nape of her neck. She might have been mistaken for a cloistered nun.

John and Sheila Goldman, Bill and June Harrington, and Helen O'Connor were convened behind them. On the opposite aisle were Vince Fredericks and several other people Ralph didn't recognize. There were six men and four women, all about Alfred's age, training faculty from the Institute, Ralph imagined. In the back there was another woman with a wide brimmed hat, heavily veiled. She held a lace handkerchief to her face. A celebrity, perhaps? A man sat next to her holding her hand with both of his. He looked familiar, too. Some actor Ralph couldn't place.

One seat over was a young film director, famous enough to be recognized. To the side, other mourners blended in. With all the publicity, Ralph was amazed to realize how few were in attendance. Ralph's attention returned to the front of the chapel, where Daniel Collins was taking the podium, thanking Donaldson for his moving eulogy, adding his sentiments to those already voiced by his elder.

Ralph was struck by how vacuous the words were. They didn't capture the essence of the man he thought he had known, or the man he was beginning to come to recognize. Ralph wondered if his memories of his former therapist had been wildly idealized. Had he created a savior in his mind to protect him through the many years of emotional turbulence? It was not an idea he cared to mull over for very long.

He tuned back into the service, just in time for Collins' logistical announcement. Mourners were to congregate at the burial site south of the chapel. Afterward they would be received by the family at their home.

The funeral had been unremarkable, as funerals go.

Later, Ralph found Randall Hart at the Merrill home outside in the garden, all alone, smoking a cigarette. "Doctor Hart," Ralph said, displaying his badge. "Detective Orloff. Beverly Hills Police. I wonder if I might have a word or two.

"Uh, sure Detective. What can I do for you?"

"I understand that you were in training with Doctor Merrill."

"That's right."

"It must be a difficult time for you, losing your analyst so suddenly."

"Well yes, as a matter of fact."

"And I'd imagine it might pose quite a handicap."

"Yes, an abrupt termination usually is, but . . .." Hart lost concentration, his eyes darting about in search of a way out. He patted his jacket and fumbled with his pack of cigarettes, finally managing to recover a lighter from a vest pocket.

"What do you do now?" Ralph said. "Just curious."

"It's really not that clear. He knew me so well," Hart said pensively, taking a long drag off his cigarette. "It's difficult to think about the prospect of starting in with someone else. I mean, it takes so long for someone to really get to know you. I've already satisfied my didactic requirement for analysis. So, I was thinking maybe I'd just wait a while. I really don't know. But I don't see how this is relevant for your investigation," Hart said defensively.

"Graduating soon?" Ralph asked, ignoring Hart's protest.

"Well yes. Soon enough. It's my last year," Hart stated proudly.

"In the home stretch, huh? Not much can stop you now."

"Stop me? Not a chance," Hart replied, turning away to crush his cigarette in a nearby flowerpot.

"I understand your office is in the same building as Doctor Merrill's," Ralph said.

"Yes, as a matter of fact, it is," Hart said with a hint of defiance.

"And were you working last Friday?"

"Of course," he exclaimed, seemingly surprised by the question and the accusation implied by it. "I was with patients, straight through until five."

"And afterwards?"

"Gee, I really can't remember. Let me think," Hart said, floundering.

Ralph began to wonder if he was onto something, until Hart regained his memory.

"Oh yes. After I closed-up my office, I went for a work-out. I was at the Sports Connection until after seven-thirty. In fact, I was with my trainer, Conrad Wendt, adjusting my routine. Then a spinning class." Hart shuffled his feet, looking straight down. "I saw him at noon, you know, Alfred I mean." Hart glanced at Ralph. "He was fine. I mean, like always."

"Which is to say?"

"Tough," Hart replied, with a spontaneity that took both men by surprise. "I didn't mean that the way it sounded. He wasn't really tough. Just no-nonsense. I mean, he pulled no punches. He called the shots just the way he saw them. He was frank, forthright." Acting as if he were caught in a snare, Hart confided, "Look Detective, Orloff was it?"

"Was and is, Doctor Hart."

"He saw me for what I am, I suppose," Hart said.

"Uh-huh."

"We all need someone who can do that and not run away, you know?"

"Uh-huh."

"He had me pegged, knew what I was. Alright?"

"And what is that Doctor Hart?"

"A very privileged, spoiled brat, who cares for no one and nothing but himself. Look, Orloff," Hart said somewhat angrily. "What is this, anyway? Am I under suspicion or something? Because if I am, I'll call my attorney, if you don't mind. I'm not used to being intimidated by those I support with my taxes when it's clear there's a real murderer out there somewhere. And I expect that his trail is growing colder every day, while you expend taxpayer's funds as well as your efforts and energies here, harassing Alfred's family, friends, and associates. We are all-law abiding citizens."

"Oh? Is that so, Doctor Hart?" Ralph countered skeptically. "Then perhaps you can tell me how such a law-abiding citizen as yourself came by that handicapped placard you use to park out in front of your office."

"What, well, I . . .,"

"You seem to be quite healthy to me," Ralph added. "Good day, Doctor Hart. And don't worry, you won't be harassed any further. That is, not unless your story fails to check out." Ralph turned to go back inside the house. Then, stopping at door, he looked back. "Oh, and Doctor Hart?"

"Yes, Detective?" Hart started.

"I'd think twice about using that handicapped permit again. Someone just might lodge a complaint someday, if you know what I mean." Ralph went inside, closing the glass slider behind himself.

He caught up with Ben, who nodded and said, "See you had a chat with Hart, eh?"

"Yeah, we talked. He's got an alibi. We'll check it out, of course, but I get the impression that our Doctor Hart is a jackal, not a lion."

"That seems like a fair assessment. So where do we go from here, Ralph?"

"We, that is you and I, had better get over to see Jerry. It's nearly five."

"Is something happening at five?"

As Ralph brought Ben up to date about Jerry, Claudine approached the two detectives. Ralph greeted her and asked, "And where will you be later, Claudine?"

"I will be here for a while longer. You know, Lucienne is so eager for the murderer be found. So upset thinking that any one of these people that she knows and whom she and Alfred had trusted may have somehow been involved. She cannot bear much more of this." Claudine attempted to collect herself. "I'm rambling on, but I just want you to know that I would like to help more if I may."

Taking her hand between his own two, Ralph said, "What if I call you after we catch up with Jerry. Perhaps, we can take you up on your offer; I may just be able to think of something you can do to help."

CHAPTER 17

Jerry's Revelation and a Ride to the Beach

Ben and Ralph found Jerry moonwalking out in front of the Roxbury building as they drove up at five o'clock sharp. As soon as he caught sight of the two detectives, he dropped his boom box down from his shoulder to his side and strolled over to the car, leaning in to speak with the two officers.

"Howdy, folks! What a fine day for a drive in a convertible. You coppers really lead the life of Riley. Now the question is, whose life does Riley live," Jerry asked, with a roar of laughter, twirling around on one foot.

"Okay, let's cut the jive, Jerry," Ben said. "This is Detective Orloff. He's the senior detective you wanted to talk to, so say what you have to say.,"

"Yessir, Detective Hollinger, Sir." Jerry saluted as he clicked his heels together. "It's just like I told the lady shrink this morning. I done read in the papers that Doc Merrill got his throat cut right up there in his very own private office." Jerry pointed upward toward the building behind them and went back to moonwalking.

"And?" Ben was impatient.

"I just thought you should know that he and a certain young lady were gettin' it on pretty good at the Trattoria Othello 'round the corner, when I was in there a few weeks back. They, that is the Doc and this nice-looking blond chick, used to have lunch there a whole lot. She, the blond that is, used to go into his office building and about an hour or so later they'd come outta there together. The look of love was in her eyes, alright. That is until recently."

"Just how recently, Jerry?" Ralph said.

"Oh, I'd say 'bout three months. Then all of a sudden-like, I didn't see her 'round no more. That is, not until last month. That's when she turned up and I see'd them in the restaurant. Havin' a lover's quarrel, they were. A terrible row. He sounded like he was wantin' somethin' from her purdy bad. But she kept sayin' *over your dead body*. Then she walked out and I ain't see'd her 'round here since."

"And you could identify this young woman if you saw her?" Ben asked.

"Yup. And ya know what," he whispered. "I 'kin do one better than that, too."

"And what's that?"

"The Doc. He was curs'n her somethin' terrible that day. And then he said *We will just see what he has to say about his darling Melissa when he hears the truth about you, Doctor Mills*. I remember what he said because I was so sur-prised to hear that this chic was a doctor. I mean, from the look of 'er, I would a thought she was a fashion model or a movie star or a fancy call girl. She was a looker alright. With her long blond hair and that fine fig'r and all," Jerry said, hoping from one foot to the other and shaking his hands out.

"Melissa Mills," Ralph repeated as Ben took notes. "Thanks Jerry. You did the right thing, telling us what you observed. One of us will get back to you with a photo to identify if this pans out. But if you don't mind my asking you, what *were* you doing in Trattoria Othello that day, the day Doctor Merrill and this woman had the argument?"

"Well sir, I went inside to use the phone and the head, like I sometimes do. The bartender, Fredo's his name, he's a real cool cat, and it was kinda warm, so he offered me a drink of water. He heard it, too. The fight. You can ask him. He'll tell it like it was."

As Jerry walked away, boom box alongside his head, Ralph turned to his partner. "Let's get on this one, right away."

Two hours later Ralph took Ben's call at the office. Ben had obtained positive identification of a photo of Mills from Jerry as well as from Fredo, the bartender in Trattoria Othello. Fredo confirmed Jerry's story, adding his own impression that the altercation between Mills and Merrill had been on the order of a lover's quarrel.

Clearly, they had frequented the cafe for lunch on a regular basis for many months, and Fredo had often overheard romantic declarations and references to love and to lovemaking exchanged between the two. But on the day of this last luncheon, Fredo was certain that he'd also heard the word *abortion* several times. He also thought he recalled hearing the name of a third doctor.

"A Jewish name," Ben said. "Maybe Glassman or Grossman. No. Goldman."

Ralph got in his car. As far as he was concerned, driving through the McClure Tunnel was one of few pleasures afforded LA's seven million motorists. It was one hundred and twenty yards of conduit linking the westbound I-10 freeway and the northbound Pacific Coast Highway. Emerging out of that 4-lane cylinder, as it bears to the right just north of the Santa Monica Pier, one is inevitably surprised by the first glimpse of the Pacific Ocean in all its sapphire splendor.

This vista spanned nearly a quarter mile before its inevitable obstruction by the assortment of private homes and restaurants huddled together along the sandy beach portion of the Southern California coastline stretching past Malibu.

It was an incomparable time of the day for a drive to the beach. With the setting sun shining, at this angle the waters sparkled.

The skies were clear and blue, decorated by just a few cottony wisps of clouds, already beginning to turn various shades of pink. An unseasonably cool and early breeze drifted over the pristine shores.

Melissa Mills was one of those fortunate residents whose home was located on that narrow patch of land between Ocean Front Walk and the bike path winding along the sand, some distance from the waters.

Ralph made a U-turn just past the Arizona overpass, pulling into the public parking lot a few yards north of Mills' address. He rang the bell at the gate and was buzzed through. The clapboard house was brightly painted, like a Mondrian canvas, with each surface and shape saturated by yet another garish hue.

Doctor Mills opened the door. In contrast to her funeral attire, she wore jeans rolled up to the knees and an overly long *Eco-Dive* tee shirt. Her hair fell loose and mussed about her shoulders, and she was scrub-faced, more alluring than she had been with cosmetic adornment.

Ralph greeted her and asked if he might put a few questions to her. Coolly agreeing, she ushered him into her living room. The typical beach house colors, pale corals and blues with splashes of sand, adorned the casual rattan-furnishings that filled the space, with its wide windows opening onto a weathered wooden terrace with striped canvas lounge chairs, a matching awning, and divorced by a diminutive glass and wrought-iron table. Finally, when they were settled, Ralph said, "I need to ask you about your relationship with Alfred Merrill."

She immediately bristled. "I don't see how this has anything to do with me," Mills protested. "I was in supervision with Doctor Merrill, but that's all. I'd have no reason to murder him," she said.

"Not even for revenge?"

"Revenge for what?"

"I understand you recently underwent an abortion," he bluffed.

Mills was unfazed. "What business is that of yours? Or anyone else's, for that matter?"

"Not even the father of the baby?"

"Not even him."

"Tell me, Doctor Mills. Wasn't it true that Alfred Merrill was the father of the baby you aborted recently?"

"I find your questions insulting and irrelevant."

He thought to himself that the District Attorney might find his questions relevant and to the point, especially when it became known that Doctor Merrill was aware of Mills' pregnancy and that he had insisted that she terminate it.

Mills' eyes had grown bloodshot with fury. She spoke as if she could read Ralph's mind. "He didn't insist on the abortion. I did." She froze, immediately realizing what she'd just admitted.

"You did, Doctor Mills?"

"I wouldn't honor him with a child. Not after what he. . . ."

She was interrupted by a door opening behind her from the bedroom, just behind and to her left. Ralph was baffled to see Kurt Cross walk through the door off the living room. He sauntered over and protectively placed his arm around Melissa's shoulder. "Whoa there, Detective Orloff. All these raised voices make me wonder what's going on in here."

"It's alright, Kurt." As she gently released herself from Kurt's protective embrace, she said,

"I may as well bring it all out in the open. I *was* having an affair with Alfred. But I ended it when I realized how neurotically motivated it really was. It was shortly after that I met Kurt. Or perhaps I should say that I met him again."

"You'd met previous to the break-up with Merrill?"

"Yes. We had been introduced when I was attending Alfred's clinical seminar at a summer party at his house."

Another summer party, another younger woman student. Same MO.

"Kurt and I met when I had a blow-out in one of my tires coming over the hill in the Canyon. He stopped to help me out, but I only had one of those mini spares to put on my wheel. So afterwards, he followed me down to a tire dealer on Pico and helped me pick out a new one. Sounds silly, but I was pretty shaken-up at the time. You see, when the tire blew, I nearly went off the road at the curve. "Kurt was sweet. I asked him home for a drink and he stayed for dinner."

"We've been dating ever since, Detective Orloff," Kurt added, smiling boyishly at Melissa. Melissa returned Kurt's regard, then continued, "It wasn't until later, almost a month later and about a week after Kurt and I became seriously involved, that a home test confirmed that I was pregnant. It was surely Alfred's baby."

"And you didn't want to carry it to term."

"No, I did not! I knew at once what I'd do. I immediately made an appointment with Leonard Grossman, my O-B-G-Y-N. His test confirmed my own and we made an appointment for a D and C the following Friday afternoon." Melissa paused, letting out an immense sigh.

All at once, Ralph recalled Merrill's files and he suddenly anticipated what would follow when she resumed her story.

"I hadn't known then that Len was in analysis with Alfred. He must have said something on the couch, about having a patient who was an analyst and upon whom he scheduled to perform an abortion."

"Small world," Ralph commented.

"Very. Alfred must have put two and two together and guessed the patient was me. Then, he called and asked if he could meet with me for lunch. He said he had something to discuss with me. Sounded quite innocent. Something about some paperwork for a case I had had in supervision with him. So, I agreed to the meeting."

"You did meet with Doctor Merrill?"

"Yes. We met around the corner from the office at Trattoria Othello on little Santa Monica. Our lunch had just been served when he began, quite inoffensively. First with small talk about young physicians in his practice. Gossip, really. He liked to do that and, I'm somewhat ashamed to say that I never had the courage or even the will to stop him. Then he really took me off guard, saying that he was surprised I would choose someone as green as Leonard Grossman for my personal physician. I was confused."

"He was playing with you."

"Yes. Like a cat with a cornered mouse. When I asked him what he was getting at, he blasted me with absolutely no regard for the fact that we were in a public place."

"He raised his voice."

"That is an understatement. He was livid, furious that I hadn't told him about the baby. He called me every name in the book. "Then, to top it off, he insisted that I have the baby and give it his name. He said that I owed it to him. Can you just imagine that for a minute?" Mills was nothing less than incensed, as if in talking about it, the whole scene was happening anew. "I told him to go to hell and left the restaurant in a terrible state. I was shocked and humiliated by his behavior. That was all."

"You mean, you just left it there?"

"Yes. I was damned if I was going to let him intimidate me."

"You had the abortion?"

"*Of course,* I had the abortion. And I never heard a word from him about it afterward. That is, not until I received a note from him in the mail last week."

"A note?"

"It arrived on Wednesday. I thought he must be deranged, out of his mind."

"Why was that?"

"Because he wrote that he knew about me and Kurt. He said that he was planning to tell Kurt the truth about us, the baby, and the abortion if I refused to come back to him. If he couldn't have me, then no one could. The bastard!"

Ralph felt slowly turned upside-down and inside-out by the emerging picture of Merrill as a jealous, possessive, and spiteful old man attempting to control all those around himself, just to preserve a deflating, grandiose bubble of self-importance.

"Of course, Kurt already knew everything," she said, rising to her feet to stand by Kurt. He placed his arm around her tiny waist, leaving no doubt in Ralph's mind that these two young people were devoted to one another. "I understood that we could never hope to make a go of our relationship with Kurt so close to Alfred and Lucienne, unless I was completely candid right from the start," Melissa explained. "I had nothing to lose that I wouldn't lose anyway if I didn't tell Kurt the truth. But do you want to know something ironic? Despite all he tried to do to me, I still felt sorry for Alfred. He was quite pathetic and lonely, you know. I think it truly drove him mad at the end. You see, Detective Orloff, I didn't kill him. I had no reason to kill him. But if he was that provocative with me, perhaps he provoked someone else as well. Someone who did have something to lose."

CHAPTER 18

Contemplating Dreams, Living Nightmares

"Claudine? It's Ralph Orloff."

"Yes Ralph, where are you? You sound very far away."

"I'm in my car, headed into town from the beach."

"The beach? What were you doing there?"

"I've been interviewing Melissa Mills."

"Melissa? But why, about what?"

"It's a long story. I'll tell you about it later when I see you."

"Are you on your way here?" Claudine asked.

Ralph noted her enthusiasm but clarified. "No. Not tonight, I'm afraid. I have to do some thinking on this and I'm better off alone right now. But I haven't forgotten what you said today, about wanting to help. I promise I'll get back with you tomorrow. "

"But of course, Ralph."

Ralph hoped that the disappointment he heard in her voice had as much to do with not seeing him as with not being able—at least for the moment—to help in the search for Merrill's murderer.

"Tomorrow then," Ralph concluded.

"Yes, of course. Good evening, Ralph."

There was a short silence before she hung up.

* * *

It had been an extremely long day. Ralph's thoughts continued to swell as he laid his head down on the pillow next to Custer's purring orange mass. Closing his eyes in the dark, Ralph pictured Claudine. He felt a warmth flow over him as he gradually lost consciousness.

Mathias Donaldson was standing, lecturing in front of Ralph as he sat at his desk in what looked like an old-style schoolroom. On the blackboard the words 'echo' and 'vexet Minerva' were written in red block letters. 'Who can tell me the significance of these terms?' Donaldson asked the class, looking down at Ralph. Someone in the back of the room spoke up, but Ralph couldn't turn around to see who it was. It sounded like Alfred's voice behind him.

Suddenly, Ralph was lying in a supine position on his back, looking up at the acoustical ceiling, not on a couch but on a scaffold suspended in the air. The dots in the ceiling had been connected and appeared to form the beginnings of a sketch, a fresco of some sort.

In the center, a male figure was pointing to an angel, female, dark-haired, falling out of the clouds. Ralph tried to catch her, but she slipped through his arms. By the time he saw that it was his daughter, Judy, falling, he could no longer right himself on the scaffolding, and she was gone.

When he awoke from his deep sleep in a fog of helplessness, his face contorted, wet with tears.

He glanced over at the clock by the side of the bed.

Six-thirty already.

The second scene in the dream was fresh, yet frozen, as though petrified like stone in his mind's eye. He was reminded of the Sistine Chapel in the Vatican. The chapel had recently been restored, but some said the restoration had spoiled the original beauty of the frescoes, they would never be the same.

So, what about that?

He thought about Judy in Italy. She hadn't telephoned from Rome as she'd said she would. He was worried. Had she been offended that he hadn't tried to reach her? Was that all that had been evoked by the dream? Was the dream merely a manifestation of his anxiety and guilt about Judy, about missing her call? He conjured up her adorable face and petite frame as he continued his train of thought. The angel of his dream looked like a different young woman, though. Not Judy, although the dark hair bore resemblance.

Giuliana Giacchini came to mind. The word *echo* and the phrase *vexet Minerva* sprang up front and center, and Ralph fleetingly recalled the dream he'd had some days before, and his conversation with Giancarlo Giacchini.

Who was Echo? Wasn't she the one who'd fallen in love with Narcissus? Was that another myth? Narcissus didn't see her, only his own reflection in a pool of water. And she wasted away without really being seen, without being loved, until finally, only her voice remained. She was merely an echo of her former self.

But Giuliana Giacchini's sparkling soprano voice did not remain. It was gone. Only an echo, a fading memory. Ralph recalled his conversation with Giancarlo about the Goddess, Minerva. *She is as mind cut off from body, civilization without mother nature's wisdom, out of touch with the earth and without common sense.*

Intellect without intuition.

Ecco. Right on, that's what it means in Italian!

Vexet Minerva.

Sounds like vexed Minerva, angry Minerva.

Of course, she'd be angry. *Her voice had been reduced to an echo after the cancer.*

Revenge. Patricide?

Think, Orloff.

The phrase, *Vexet Minerva. Isn't it meant to express a sense that something or someone is so stupid or thoughtless, or some act so pointless, that it angers the Goddess of Intellect,* who is also the *Goddess of War?*

Ralph's mind raced back to his interview with Giuliana.

Why did you interrupt your analysis with Doctor Merrill, against medical advice?

Because he did not understand me, Detective Orloff. It's as simple and as complicated as that. Doctor Alfred Merrill simply did not see me at all. In fact, he completely underestimated me.

She had said that he didn't see her. She had wasted away from her cancer, until only an echo of her former voice remained. *But what did this have to do with Alfred's murder? And why was Donaldson in the dream?* The conversation at the funeral, what was it he'd said?

One kills someone . . . they know and love, perhaps a lover or spouse or even a relative . . . these people invariably have isolated-out, from their conscious awareness, years of grievances and the feelings associated with such grievances . . . defensively cordoned-off from consciousness . . . these aspects of experience take on a life of their own . . . they fester and grow like a cancer.

Like a cancer.

Could it be that Giuliana Giacchini, overwhelmed by grievances transferred from the past and resonating with those in the present, had murdered her former analyst?

After a moment of indecision, Ralph reached for the telephone by the side of the bed. He hoped it wasn't too early to call Claudine. She could help him. She wanted to—and she was the only one who *could* help him to think it through. Even so, he could feel the resistance within himself as he punched in her number.

Damn!

Ralph slammed the phone down before it began to ring. Then he threw his legs over the side of the bed, barely missing Custer, who was diving for cover under the dust ruffle.

Damn!

Ralph cursed, as he pulled off his tee-shirt and shorts and

threw them across the room, heading for the shower to stall for time. The hot water felt good, encouraging truth to flow into his conscious mind as it woke up his body. How he'd like to be calling her for a date, not for a consult on a murder case. She was just about everything he was attracted to in a woman. Dignified, feminine, intelligent, quick witted, sensitive and lovely to look at. As Ralph reached for the towel, he heard the telephone ringing. *It might be Judy*, he thought as he hurried to beat the machine.

"Hello?"

"Ralph," Claudine sounded relieved. "I'm so glad I could reach you. I was concerned you might have left already. Could we please meet?"

"Of course," Ralph said, trying his best to contain his curiosity and exhilaration. "In fact, I was about to call you. I'd like to run something by you, and I don't think the telephone is the place for it. Why don't I come by your place, say in about an hour?"

"Yes. Yes, that would work well. Have you had anything for breakfast yet?"

"Not yet. Can I pick up something on my way?"

"Not necessary. I have croissants and I can make some scrambled eggs if you like. See you soon."

Sitting at Claudine's kitchen table, bathed in the warmth of morning while she poured the coffee, Ralph told her about the encounter with Jerry, the conversation with Fredo, the subsequent interview with Melissa Mills, and the dream he had recalled from that morning.

"You know, I have a hunch that Giuliana Giacchini is in this thing up to her pretty little neck," Ralph said. "You see? There I go again. My unconscious is leading, all the way."

"It is remarkable," Claudine exclaimed. "Especially when I tell you that I was calling you this morning because I, too, have come across some disturbing evidence that may point to Giulia's involvement in Alfred's death."

"Really? Please."

"Last night, after I returned home from Lucienne's, after you called me, Giulia rang. She was weeping. She'd taken an overdose of Halcion, a sleeping medication, when she returned home after the funeral. She was frightened that she might die. She was afraid to let Giancarlo know. She didn't wish to worry him, so she called me instead."

"But why you?"

"I was a very close friend of her mother's. Or perhaps I had not told you. In any case, I drove over there at once."

"Was it a suicide attempt?"

"No. Not at all. She had only swallowed six tablets. At most she would have slept through the next day, which might have worried Gianni to death. And he would have been furious with her when she woke up. Primarily, I believe that Giulia wanted me to reassure her that she had not done irreparable damage to herself, so I went to her immediately."

"Sounds like she felt persecuted, poor kid."

"Well, she was quite confused and drowsy when I arrived. She babbled on about Alfred."

"What did she say?"

"That he had it coming to him. That it was too late for her, but not too late for Michael."

"Do you know what she meant?"

"I had no idea, so I asked. But she just repeated over and over again *never mind, never mind,* and she cried her eyes out. She murmured something about how her father had never loved her, she was only a bird in a gilded cage. That she could never fly away because he'd die without her."

"Make sense to you?"

"No, not at all. Then she uttered something about her mother, how she had left them, how Giancarlo had told her that she was *just like her mother* ever since she was very, very little. Ever since she could recall."

"Her mother died when she was a baby, I take it," Ralph said.

"When she was born, in fact. Sophia died in childbirth."

"Gee, that's rough!"

"Yes, it was. It was the year after they had moved here from Italy. The delivery came quite unexpected, too quickly for everyone. Sophia was all alone when she went into labor, nearly a month prematurely. We were all with our patients when it happened. She called Gianni and then me, instead of her obstetrician or an ambulance. You see, her English was not very good, and she was inhibited to speak. She began hemorrhaging so severely, and she lost consciousness before help could arrive."

"But the baby was alright."

"Giuliana was delivered quite miraculously. When Gianni came home earlier than usual due to a last-minute cancellation, he found Sophia on the floor, bleeding and unconscious. She had nearly exsanguinated, but her baby girl was alright. That is, as soon as Giancarlo cut away the tangled umbilical cord that was wrapped tightly around her throat, like a noose. Tragically it was too late for Sophia. She died in the ambulance on the way to the hospital."

"What a nightmare," Ralph said, shaking his head.

"Yes. And I'm afraid that the nightmare is not yet over with."

Ralph looked at her and winced. Her grief was evident. "I don't like having to involve you in this, Claudine," he said. "I know it must be difficult, but I need your help to sort some things out. Here's what we have. First, Giuliana Giacchini was one of the few people who knew that Michael Pearlman was out of town and had canceled his hour with Merrill. She knew that Alfred would be alone. Second, her whereabouts at the time of the murder is questionable. She said she was alone in her room, which makes her alibi non-verifiable. Third, she knew the deceased and certainly had reason to harbor a grudge. And it would seem, at least from what you're telling me now, that she may have had a deep-seated motive."

Claudine gasped, as she burst into tears. "Oh Ralph, I can hardly even bear the thought of it. The possibility that Giulia could do such a thing. But there is something else I have not yet mentioned." Claudine struggled with her escalating anguish. "It's just that I was remembering what the coroner said to you about the murderer. I recall that he said that the perpetrator used a small, extremely sharp implement, a scalpel or a straight razor. Very sharp, held in the left hand. Well. . ." Claudine hesitated.

"Go on," Ralph prodded.

"Ralph, Giuliana *is* left-handed. And one thing more. When I went into Giulia's bathroom to get her a glass of water and to check the bottle of Halcion to see how many tablets were left, I saw, I saw a scalpel."

"Where?"

"It was in the medicine cabinet. I took both the bottle and the scalpel with me." Claudine reached into her purse on the chair beside her. She gently lifted out and unfolded a packet wrapped in some tissue, revealing the gleaming stainless-steel instrument, laying it on the table between them. "Could this be the murder weapon?" she asked, trembling and holding herself, her slender arms crisscrossed against her breasts.

"Could be. Did you handle it at all?"

"Only with the tissue."

"That's good. Now, take a deep breath. I need one more thing from you, Claudine." He placed his hand over hers as she held onto him with her eyes. "Do you have a photograph of Giuliana? One I could borrow for a while? I'd like to show it to some people before we go any further with this."

"Of course, I have, but . . ."

"No questions now, please. Just get me the photo. We're gonna have to take a little ride if you want to come with me."

Claudine excused herself and went to her bedroom. A minute later she returned and handed Ralph a snapshot of Giulia in street clothes, surrounded by exotic gowns, apparently taken in a theater's dressing room. Claudine's look of longing spoke volumes. Clearly she did not wish to be alone.

Ralph drove up Little Santa Monica until they saw Jerry standing in front of the men's-only specialty gift shop near the corner of Camden. Ralph turned the corner, stopped the car and got out, just as Jerry turned and saw him.

"Hey man, back again?"

"Just wanna ask you one more question, Jerry."

"Hit me, baby."

"Do you recall the conversation you had with Detective Hollinger the other day?"

"The other day," he repeated, scratching his hooded head.

"You said that you'd seen someone last Friday that you hadn't seen for about two years. Someone who used to visit the building on Roxbury daily. Someone with dark, wavy hair, down her back, smooth skin, nice bod, a real dazzler. Someone you said you might be able to identify if you saw her again?"

"Yeah, man. I recollect 'dat all right. I said I could, and I can. So, what about 'er?"

"Take a look at this photo and tell me if this is the woman you saw entering the Roxbury Building last Friday afternoon."

Jerry put down his boom box and removed his sunglasses as he took the photograph from the detective. "Right on, man! That's herself, aw'right," he said with a lecherous grin. "Now it all comes back to me. She was wear'in one of them body stockings, a cat suit. And big dark glasses, too. And she had this raincoat she carried over one arm. I remember now. Thought it was funny, seein' as how there weren't a cloud in the sky, and it was a hot one, yes it was. But then, I don't have to tell you that," he said, slapping Ralph on the shoulder.

Then he pointed toward the brick building to clarify. "She went right into that buildin'. Same one where that Doc was murdered t'other day, wasn't it?" Scratching his beard, Jerry said, "Hey, you don't think maybe she was the one done it, do ya?"

"Thanks Jerry. You've been a big help. Keep up the good work," Ralph said, ignoring the question, slapping the man on his shoulder. Returning to his car, Ralph slid into the seat next to Claudine.

Feeling her anxiety, he pre-empted her question. "One more place to go, I'm afraid. Can you bear with me?"

"Of course," Claudine sighed. "But where are we going?"

"We're going to the Goldmans'. I need to see Rachael. I don't think you want to go there with me, do you? You might want to wait in your office."

A bit annoyed, she did not move. "I could wait in the car, but why Rachael?" When he hesitated, she simply said, "Okay." With disappointment and resignation, she released her seat belt. "I'll wait for you here at my office."

Ralph looked at her. Contemplating the possibility that she didn't really want to be alone, he softened. "Look, I don't see why you can't wait in the car, if you like. Besides, I'd enjoy the company. *Your* company."

"Will you tell me why afterward, why you went there?" she asked.

"If it's relevant, yes. I promise I will."

"Let's be on our way then."

They rode the few blocks in charged silence, arriving at the Goldman residence to find the yellow Corvette parked on the street in front of the house. Ralph pulled over and parked in front of it, got out and walked up to the door and knocked.

Minutes later he exited the house, got into the driver's seat, and stared straight ahead. Then he started the car and headed toward Roxbury Drive.

Finally, Claudine said, "I can't stand this, Ralph. Will you please tell me what is going on?"

"Let's go to your office and I'll lay it all out for you."

As soon as they entered Claudine's office building, right there in the lobby, Ralph began to explain. "When I spoke with her on Saturday, Rachael Goldman had mentioned that when she came into the building to see you on Friday afternoon, she was in a hurry, late for her session. But she had noticed a woman at the pay phone, just as the elevator door closed."

He pointed. "This payphone." He walked over to the phone that hung on the wall near the pharmacy. "Rachel said that the woman looked as if she'd been crying. She said that she thought she looked familiar, too, with long dark hair, very upset."

"What are you telling me?

"That Rachel just identified this photograph of Giuliana Giacchini as the woman on the phone," Ralph said, producing the snapshot.

"But Ralph. Does that necessarily mean that Giulia . . .?"

"Claudine, I'm afraid it looks bad. Jerry also identified the photo. He saw Giulia entering this building last Friday afternoon. He recognized her as the same woman who, until a couple of years ago, had visited this building nearly every weekday."

Sensitive to Claudine's shock, he reached for her hand and held it firmly. They stepped into the elevator together. Ralph turned toward Claudine, looking into her eyes as he continued. "I know how fond you must be of Giuliana, but I'm going to have to extend my investigation of her possible involvement in Alfred Merrill's murder."

Ralph could see the tears welling up again in her eyes. "Oh Ralph," Claudine struggled for breath, as the fear she'd been concealing from herself penetrated her awareness. Within the privacy of her own consulting room, Claudine sat next to Ralph on the couch, sobbing for a long time, her head on his shoulder. He became aware that this was the first time he had seen her actually lose control of her emotions. He wanted to comfort her, but he felt like the enemy. Nonetheless, as he encircled her in his arms, she relaxed all the more into his shoulder, clinging to him as if he were an old friend.

As her tears subsided, Claudine looked up at his face. Ralph wondered what she saw there. Could she be attracted to him? He hoped she might recognize his mounting affection for her. This woman he'd known for less than a week had captured his heart, and now he was breaking hers. Even so, she reached up with a gentle hand, touching his cheek.

"Thank you. Thank you for allowing me some time to deal with this. You *are* a friend," she said.

"I would like to be, Claudine."

"It seems I truly need one. I haven't felt so alone since Bernard died. You see," she said, as she pulled herself upright, smoothing her clothing and drying her eyes, "He was my best friend," she said. "As well as my husband and my lover."

Ralph could feel the bond between them growing. How alike they were. Each having lost a mate, a best friend, a great love. He wanted to tell her, but it was not the time. Not until this mess was cleared away, once and for all.

They sat close together like that for some minutes, until Claudine asked him, "Will you be placing Giuliana under arrest now?"

"I think it would be best to have a talk with her first. It might make it easier on her if we can get her to cooperate."

"You mean if she makes a confession."

"If she does, so much the better," Ralph said.

"Would it help, do you think, if I went with you when you talk with her?"

Ralph gave a brief thought to the legitimacy of the presence of a civilian in an interrogation, at this point. "It might help. But are you sure you're up to it? And is it okay, given who you are to her?"

"Yes, I think so. Besides, I wish to be with her. Perhaps I might even be able to prevail upon her to face the truth. She has been through so much in her young life."

"From what you've told me, it certainly seems so. And unfortunately, it looks like there may be more to come, if she has to stand trial."

"All the more reason for me to be there then. She may need me now more than ever."

As Ralph and Claudine pulled up in front of the Giacchini

home, Ralph noticed that Claudine looked uneasy. "Look, if you've changed your mind, Claudine, it's O.K." he said. "I'll call Ben and take you home."

"No Ralph, I've not changed my mind. I just sense something is wrong."

"Wrong?"

"Yes, wrong. At first I thought that perhaps it was our decision not to call Giuliana before returning to talk with her."

"Well, we can correct that one right now. You can call her on the cellular before we—"

"No. I realized it's not really that," Claudine stammered, with a perplexed look that Ralph had come to recognize.

"Well, we now know what it's not. Any clue as to what it is?"

"I thought, maybe we should talk to Giancarlo first. Maybe that is why I am feeling so. . ." she paused, once again in thought.

"No," he said. "She's an adult."

"Oh, I know. And it is not that either. Never mind me. I am just postponing the inevitable."

They walked together to the entry of the house. As usual, it was a convivial Giancarlo who opened the door. "Cara Claudia, Detective Orloff. What an unexpected pleasure to see the two of you together," Giacchini said, winking at Ralph. "Please, come in."

"Thank you, Gianni," Claudine said, as they entered the house. "We've really come to speak with Giulia."

"Giuliana . . .?" he repeated, with surprise. But I think that you have already talked with my daughter, Detective Orloff. There are more questions?"

"I'm afraid there are more questions, Doctor Giacchini."

"*Va bene*, then we must cooperate. I believe that my daughter is in her room just this moment. Come, we will knock her door and see if she is presentable."

He ushered them down a hallway to a closed door, where he proceeded to knock.

No response.

"I have not seen my daughter today, but I know she is here. Her car is yet in the garage." Giancarlo knocked again, while calling out. "Giuliana, we have guests."

Still no response.

Ralph glanced at Claudine. They shared a look. He sensed that they were both thinking about the same thing.

The sleeping pills.

"Is there another entrance to this room?" Ralph asked.

Giancarlo had already tried the door and, finding it locked, was now frenetically knocking a third time. "Yes, there is the door from the patio, outside in the garden," he responded, turning to lead the way down the hall and out onto the patio through the master suite.

Through the French doors, the three of them could see clearly inside Giuliana's room. The white-tiled floor of the skylit bathroom was in plain sight. On the floor lay Giuliana Giacchini, her dark curls soaking in the deep red stain that was rapidly spreading through the open doorway.

"*Madonna Santa!*" Giancarlo cried out.

Horrified, he glanced over at Ralph for a moment. As Claudine looked on with disbelief, the two men, as if sharing a single thought, aimed their respective right shoulders toward the junction of the wood-framed glass doors, thrusting at them with the full weight of their bodies.

As they burst into the room, Giancarlo rushed to his daughter, lying nearly lifeless on the floor, clad only in taupe lace panties and a camisole. Ralph looked around and swiftly grabbed towels off the racks. The two men worked together, tying a tourniquet on the delicate wrist, which appeared to have been sliced open vertically with a shard of the mirror that had once covered the medicine cabinet. Claudine was already on the telephone at the dressing table, dialing 911 for an ambulance. She raced into the bathroom with a blanket and pillows pulled from the bed, propping up Giuliana's feet and covering her nearly naked body against the chill of shock.

When the paramedics arrived, Giuliana was barely breathing. There was a flurry of activity. Within minutes she was stabilized. Hooked up to an assortment of bags and bottles, they loaded her into the ambulance. Accompanied by her father, they sped off down Olympic Boulevard.

Ralph and Claudine followed close behind. Ralph switched on the car phone and hit speed dial. Ben answered on the second ring. "Don't tell me," Ben said. "Something's up."

"Ben? Meet me at the Century City Hospital Emergency Room right away. I think we're about to break the Merrill case."

"Fuck *me!* Where are you?"

"In route with Claudine."

"Be there in fifteen."

The moment Ralph switched off the phone, Claudine turned to and said, "Please, can you tell me, what will happen to Giuliana now?" They were the first words she had spoken to him since he and the girl's father had broken down the doors to Giuliana's room.

"If she pulls through?" he said. "We'll have questions. Are you alright; Do you need anything?"

"No. I feel terrible. I should have stayed with her last night, Ralph. I should have confided in Giancarlo instead of telling you. I should have . . ."

"Hold up there a minute. Take it easy on yourself, will you. You said yourself that it wasn't a serious attempt."

"I know, I know what I said. *But I was obviously wrong,*" Claudine shouted in despair and rage.

"You weren't omniscient, that's true," Ralph said gently. "But I'll give you another piece of the truth. If you hadn't told me, that girl might be on her way to the morgue right now instead of the hospital. At least now, she has a fighting chance."

"A chance of what? Of recovering from her latest suicide attempt or a chance to be charged with Alfred's murder? Oh Ralph. I am sorry. I did not mean to strike out at you, of all people." She took his hand and squeezed it tightly in hers as they pulled up to the emergency entrance. "You're right. We must get to the bottom of this, find the truth. My sweet Giuliana must be heard and seen."

CHAPTER 19

Confession and Restauration

It was nearly four in the afternoon when Giancarlo found Ralph, Ben and Claudine waiting and worrying over their fifth cup of coffee in the hospital cafeteria. They all glanced up, just as Giancarlo came through the door, looking much smaller and older than he'd appeared to them just hours before in the doorway of his home.

He was pale, drawn, and chalky, but also relieved. He sighed. "I just left her." Giacchini sounded completely broken as he pulled out the remaining chair and dropped into it, letting his head collapse into his hands, elbows on the table. "She will recover from this, from all of it. She is conscious now and asking to speak with you, Claudine."

Reaching out to take his hands, now stretched out across the table, Claudine spoke softly. "My poor Gianni. Has Giulia been able to say anything about what happened? About why she . . .?"

"No, nothing. She's crying and she says that she wants to talk to her Zia Claudia. What she needs right now is a Mama, not a Papa. Will you go to her, Cara?" Giacchini pleaded, tears filling his eyes.

"Of course, Gianni, I will go to her at once."

"I'll accompany you," Ralph said, as he rose in response to Claudine's pleading eyes. "Thanks ever so much," she replied.

"Ben, you stay here with the Doctor."

"Sure thing, partner." Ben replied.

When they opened the door of the hospital room, they saw Giuliana lying there, covered only with a sheet. Her skin was nearly as white as the bandages on her left wrist and the tape that held the IV needle in place on her right arm. Her sable mane, matted with her own dried blood, had been tied back away from her bare shoulders. Her eyelids seemed almost translucent. Her long full lashes fluttered briefly as if she were dreaming.

Claudine and Ralph nodded to the nurse, who seemed to be stationed there to monitor the patient. As Claudine sat beside her on the bed, Giuliana moved her too-pale lips and spoke. "I'm so sorry, *Zia* Claudia," she spoke in a low whisper, as she opened her expressive eyes.

"Sorry for what? Hush now, *viens ma toute petite*. You will be alright. I am here with you now, *piccinina*."

"But I have done something terrible." She limply held up her bandaged wrist. "Not just this. There is so much more."

"Yes, my darling," Claudine said. "I think we know something about what is troubling you. And there will be time for you to tell us. But first you must rest. *N'est-ce pas?*"

"You will stay with me," Giuliana murmured, as her eyelids gave way under the weight of the heavy sedative.

"Yes, *Cherie*. I will stay," Claudine promised, as she looked back at Ralph, standing at the foot of the bed.

He was nodding his head. They both knew that their questions could wait for morning. Ralph and Claudine returned to the cafeteria to say goodnight to Ben and Gianni. Then Ralph drove Claudine home for the night.

"Please come in for a nightcap," Claudine said. "We could both use one, if you think you can drive. Maybe an Irish coffee, decaffeinated of course."

"Thanks, I think I'll take the caffeine."

Ralph looked around Claudine's living room. The Louis XVI furnishings and color combinations reminded him of one trip to Paris when he and Dorothy had stayed at the Hotel Regina Louvre. Why was he always reminded of Dorothy? Would it always be that way, everything and everyplace reminding him of his life with her? Would there ever be room for another woman in his life?

After the warmth of Claudine's company, the coffee and liquor, and the sweetness of the Chantilly cream had tentatively filled his bitter emptiness, he said goodnight, wanting to pick her up on the way to the hospital for the interrogation around noon. Wanting her there as she wished to be. His eyes met hers at the door and she gave him a caress with her breath on each cheek in agreement. He almost enjoyed a dreamless, deep sleep that night.

When he and Claudine drove to the hospital the next morning, Ralph decided not to share his most urgent thoughts. He feared he was playing with fire. Giuliana did not have to speak with him, although it certainly seemed that she wanted to. He decided not to arrest her—there would plenty of opportunity for that later, if it was warranted—and to conduct an informal Q and A with whomever she wanted present—Claudine, her father, the nurse, anyone.

And he had to walk a fine line: on the one hand, she was obviously weak, in distress, and hardly able to mount a robust defense if—or, rather, when—he started asking her pointed questions. On the other, she was a patient in a hospital bed after an apparent suicide attempt, and the last thing he wanted was to bully or intimidate her.

After everyone had gotten settled—including a new nurse, for this daytime shift—and Ralph had obtained (and recorded) her consent that the session be taped, he gently broached the topic. He asked what she recalled of the events of Friday, July 30th. Giuliana Giacchini's recital contained a curious blend of rational insights and mad conclusions.

"I knew Alfred would be alone," she said. The night's rest had done her good, and she seemed less frail than when they had left her the previous evening. "I called him from the public phone in the lobby of the building and told him that I was downstairs and that I needed to see him at once."

"And that was at approximately what time?"

"Five."

"Five in the afternoon?"

"Yes."

"And he asked you up to his office?"

"Well, not exactly."

"Then what did happen when you asked to see Doctor Merrill?"

"At first he said no. That is, until I began to cry. I told him I knew he wasn't busy. That I knew Michael was away and I simply had to see him. I begged and pleaded, until finally he agreed."

"And what occurred when you went upstairs to Doctor Merrill's office?"

"When I walked into the waiting room, he was standing there with the door to the inner hallway open. He confronted me like a stern father, letting me know right off that he wouldn't put up with any of my nonsense."

"So, he confronted you right away, even before you entered his consulting room?"

"Yes, he did that."

"And just what did he say?"

"He said something like *So, Giuliana*, with nothing but disdain in his voice. *What could you possibly have to tell me that you could not have told me just as well over the telephone?*"

"And what happened next?"

"He was so insensitive. I felt enraged. It welled up in me, it was almost beyond my control. I taunted him."

"You taunted him?"

"Yes. I brushed past him into his consulting room, and I said, *I thought you psychoanalysts were just dying for the opportunity to follow-up on the impressive successes of your treatments, but I thought that surely you could only be afforded such an opportunity upon the request of the patient. Isn't that so?* And I pretended to make myself at home in one of his chairs."

"You sat down in a chair. And Merrill, what did he do?"

"I think he was curious. He came in behind me, closed and locked the door and sat down across from me in the other chair. He even admitted his interest in me. He said it was always helpful to know the outcome of an analysis. He let me know that this was not just for personal but for scientific reasons. And he asked me if that was really what I had come for."

"But that wasn't the only reason you had come to see him, was it?"

"No! It wasn't the reason at all, but I said, *In a way, Doctor Merrill. In a way I have come to show you the results of your work. But I would also like to try a scientific experiment of my own. I've always wondered what it would feel like to be in your place. To sit in your chair. And to have you lie on the couch. To change places, as it were. Then we could share in each other's perspectives more completely. Don't you think that would be an interesting experiment, Doctor Merrill?*"

"And did he go along with this, the experiment?"

"Not at first, of course. At first he gave me an interpretation . . . *It seems you can hardly bear the feeling of being the patient. Just as it is unbearable to feel like a small child, out of control, like a guinea pig in a laboratory. You wish to get rid of those feelings and to have me feel them for you by forcing them into me. And while you are letting me know how it feels to be small and powerless, like a helpless baby lying in a crib, you plan to rob me of my identity as the all-powerful-scientist-analyst-father, and you will become the one who hovers sadistically above the baby-me.*

"Then you will have become the one who neglects to help or protect or feed, just as you must have felt that I neglected you ever since the termination of your analysis."

"That was his interpretation?" Ralph said.

"Yes, I remember it clearly."

"And then what happened?"

"I said, *it won't work, Doctor*. I even smiled at him while I pulled my little pearl-handled pistol out of my handbag. I pointed it at him, and when I did that, I felt a real rush of power."

"And what did he do when you pointed the gun at him?"

"Why, he did nothing. But what could he do but watch? He was horrified. Finally, he regained his speech and stammered something indignantly."

"Something? Do you recall what he said?"

"Yes. Something like *and just what do you think you are going to do with that, that gun, young woman?*"

"And what did you do when he challenged you about the gun?"

"I almost had to laugh. He was quite comical, pathetic. But instead, I said with a perfectly straight face, *it is my most sincere hope that I won't have to use it. If only you don't make me use it. I do not wish to use it really, except to convince you to do what I say. I want you to lie on the couch.* Then he almost shouted at me, *You what? Are you crazy?*

"I assured him, *No, I am not crazy. I have something I wish to tell you, and for my own reasons, I would like you to lie on the couch while I say what I have to say.*

"Alfred replied, this time with even more indignation, *I will do no such thing.*

"Then he tried another interpretation, *you are simply trying to turn the tables on me, making me submit to your powerful will, just as you felt I . . .* but there I interrupted his feeble attempt to sway me. I told him I was certain that before I was finished, even he would see that there is more than just one interpretation for a given set of associations. *I would like to give you my interpretation,* I said. *It is for this reason that I must sit in the analyst's chair, and you must lie on the analysand's couch. Then, when I have said what I have to say, we will see who is correct. I will even let you be the judge. Is that clear?* I asked this last question, as I gestured him toward the couch with the gun, my finger right on the trigger so that he could see how serious I really was.

"Then a smile, no not a smile, a smirk really transformed his face. The fear in his expression was suddenly gone. And I had a very strong feeling that he now felt somehow that he had the upper hand. As he rose from the chair and walked to the couch, I knew I was right. It seemed that he had somehow been able to convince himself of his ultimate superiority, as usual.

"And then he lay right down on the couch without a care in the world, as if it were the most natural thing he could do. I was relieved to know that I would not have to use the gun. Oh, I was prepared to, of course. But you see, it would have spoiled everything. And the noise, well it would have been so messy, especially with you right in the next room, Zia Claudine. "But Alfred was quite cooperative, really," Giuliana said.

"Smiling, I sat in his chair, that great big dark reddish recliner behind the couch. It had always looked so imposing with him in it. But at that moment, it was just another chair. Nothing special at all.

That is, until I sat down in it. It felt so big. And, contrary to what you might think, or at least contrary to what Alfred thought, I did not feel like the all-powerful-scientist-analyst-father. I felt like a little girl. I felt like Lily Tomlin's Edith Ann as I tried to get up the steam to speak to him, my feet unable to touch the ground.

"I finally did. And I reminded him of those last months of my analysis. That period had begun with a dream I had one Sunday night. I reported it in my Monday hour. In the dream . . .

"I was in the green room, warming up backstage before a performance at the Music Center. I was excited because I had taken my mother's diamond broach to wear under my costume. The opera was La Boehme, and I was to sing the part of Mimi. But just as I began to sing the last Aria, the one when Mimi is dying, my voice died.

"I felt like there were two hands grasping at my throat, choking me from behind, but when I turned around, there was no one there. Just a big cat, grinning. A Cheshire Cat. I was frightened by its teeth.

"I ran out on the stage. I was naked and very small, like a little girl. A woman laughed in the audience, but I could not see her because the house lights had already been dimmed, and I woke up feeling frightened, humiliated and crying."

"So, you reminded him of the dream that you had," Ralph said.

"And about the associations to the dream. I reminded him that I'd recalled, at that time, that on the previous Sunday during the rehearsals that I had almost completely lost my voice for a while. I had been feeling so very tired and weak and felt a scratchy sore throat. It reminded me of a time when I was very little, only about two years old, when I had my tonsils removed. The Doctor who did the surgery—I thought that I had remembered that his name was Doctor Castrate—had very big teeth and always smiled. I thought that *he* looked like the Cheshire cat.

"After the surgery was finished, I had vomited blood in my hospital bed, and it went all over my gown and the sheets. They left me naked while they changed the linens. When the doctor came in, he and the nurse laughed at me. She said that I was a funny little thing, covering my non-existent breasts and pubic area with my little hands, as if I had something to cover up, and they both laughed even louder. I'll never forget how humiliated I felt. I was cold and mortified."

"And what was Doctor Merrill's response to this story of your tonsillectomy?"

"Alfred interpreted the dream. He insisted that my loss of voice had occurred as the result of my feeling cut-off from him and by him over that weekend. He said that I also felt him to be a castrating doctor-mother from whom I had to hide my strength and talent, my voice, so that now without my voice I was just an innocent little girl with nothing to protect from an envious mother-Doctor."

"And after you reminded him of all this, Giuliana?"

"I wanted to really make him suffer. I wanted him to see what had happened to me. That it was his fault that I would never sing again, that I would never have anything to protect again."

"His fault?" Ralph said. "Why?"

"Because he kept insisting my throat problems were psycho somatic, and that only he could cure them. And I went along with it. But they weren't psychosomatic. They were organic. And I was convinced to ignore them until it was too late."

She went on, "So I said to him, *you thought you were so clever. You never once considered the possibility that I was really sick. You were so puffed up with your own magnificence that you never once considered that my physical symptoms could have some organic basis.*

"He never suggested, even as he watched my symptoms grow worse and worse, even when I did not respond to his line of interpretation, that we might want to rule out some physical ailment. Instead, he became more and more persecutory with his interpretations, insisting that I was having a perversely negative reaction to the accuracy of his understanding of my fantasies. I added *you even insisted that I was envious of your good interpretations. You said that I was attacking them, as well as my own good voice, which you insisted was equated with your voice. You said that I wanted to still the voice of truth in you and, in my state of confusion with you, I was silencing my own voice as well. You insisted that, in my attempt to ruin your career, I was ruining my own career, too. For you, my symptoms were merely a manifestation of my own envious attack on all that was good in each of us.*"

"And what was Doctor Merrill's reaction to that?"

"He was absolutely silent at first. I thought that he knew what he had done. It was the first time I could ever recall Alfred at a loss for words. It was almost as if he had caved in on himself. Imploded. It was visible. It was palpable. He was devastated. He was speechless for a very long time. I felt exhilarated because he was struck dumb by the truth. The taste of revenge was sweet, and I wanted more. I was ready to go in for the kill.

"But then I began to feel sorry for him. He seemed so broken, lying there with tears rolling down his gaunt and aged cheeks. He looked old and weak. I got up out of the chair and looked down on him.

"For a moment I felt like I was just going to leave him there. I thought for a moment that I had had enough revenge. It was over at last," Giuliana said, as she heaved a sigh of relief.

There was a long pause while she closed her dark eyes and seemed to sink deeper into her pillow. Ralph thought for a moment that she was falling asleep. He looked at Claudine sitting next to him. She nodded and took Giuliana's hand in her own. Then, as if she were deriving some necessary substance from this physical connection, something that enabled her to continue, Giuliana opened her eyes and began to speak once again.

"It appeared to me, in that long silence, that Alfred had taken in my words, that he really grasped their meaning, their significance. I thought that, just maybe, he had let my words and my situation touch him at last. That, for once in his life, he was feeling truly remorseful.

"I was so naive that I even thought he might have learned a lesson from what had happened to me. That he might really change as a result of it. That he would never cause damage to anyone else, ever again. That his grandiosity would now be tempered with the painful realization of what it had done to me."

She sighed deeply, her eyes glistening with tears. "If only he had kept silent, it might all be different now."

"But he didn't stay silent?"

"No. As I stood there over him the color came back into his face. He seemed to reconstitute. He lay there, eyes closed, and said in that oh-so-seductive way he had, *Giuliana, dear heart, I hope you know that I would have cut my own throat had I thought for a moment that I was contributing to the loss of that wondrous and magical voice of yours. I hope you now realize how truly sorry I am.*

"It was then that I knew that nothing had moved in him in the least. He was the same old Alfred. In his silence he had not taken in the implications of my words. He had not contemplated his own culpability. He was not taking responsibility. He was abdicating any of it." Then Giuliana cried out as she lifted herself up off the pillow, taking hold of Claudine's hand with one of hers and grasping her upper arm with the other.

Ralph said, "That realization, that nothing had changed in Doctor Merrill, must have had quite an effect on you."

"Effect? I was enraged. I suddenly thought of Michael."

"Michael Pearlman, your fiancée?"

"Yes. My fiancée. I had never been able tell him why I had put off seeing a specialist about my condition until it was too late. I couldn't tell him, because it would have spoiled his own analysis and probably our relationship as well. I couldn't even tell him why I couldn't marry him. But at the same time, I couldn't risk the consequences of doing nothing."

"And what did you imagine those consequences might be?"

"I knew what would become of Michael if he stayed in analysis with Alfred. He was already starting to become another Merrill clone. I couldn't bear to see him become dogmatic like all the others. I grew up seeing it happen to other people, like Dan Collins. I had overheard my father talk about it many times. But then, Father's animosity toward Alfred only made Alfred seem more intriguing as a man at the time. It never sank in on the level of reality. It only fed my fantasies of running away with my father's rival. All the talk of the danger of his way of thinking, his way of working, had no significance for me. At least not until my own experience with Alfred drove my father's words home."

"So, you found out just how dangerous it could be."

"And then, when I did understand, when I thought about Michael being in training with him, I realized I had to do something or he would ruin Michael, just as he had ruined me. It had already begun. He was already spoiling things between the two of us.

"Michael's interest in psychosomatic medicine was only a passing fad. But it had been Alfred's passion. He had been famous for his research in the field long before becoming an analyst. And he was imposing it on Michael, urging him to take the topic up in his research. We fought about it the night before Michael went to San Francisco to give that paper. I refused to go to hear him speak. I couldn't bear to hear Alfred's words coming from my Michael's lips. To hear him working for Alfred's interests, not his own. In a way I knew that Michael could end up losing *his* voice forever, just as I had lost mine. But this time the malignancy would not be a cancer. Alfred was the malignancy. And I had to cut it out before it grew again. Before it grew in my Michael, too."

"So that's why you stayed here when Michael went to San Francisco," Ralph said. "You decided to do it that day. You went to Alfred Merrill's office with the intent to murder him."

"His eyes were still closed when I slashed the blade of that scalpel across his neck. He was so cock-sure, so much in a state of denial, that he never even seemed to register what had happened. He simply opened his eyes, a first looking surprised, angry, fearful, even humiliated. For a moment, I thought he was going to smile at me, but he just lost consciousness as he began to bleed out on the couch."

"Then what did you do?"

"I took some Kleenex from the dispenser on his desk. I had some blood on my left wrist. Alfred's blood. I wiped it off. Wiped off the scalpel. Wrapped it in the tissue and put it in my purse. I put on my raincoat and dark glasses, I sat down in the chair at his desk, and I watched him as the life completely drained out of him. I waited until six o'clock and then I let myself out."

Taking a deep breath, Ralph asked, "Ms. Giacchini, can you tell me what made you attempt suicide?"

"It was the blood."

"What blood?"

"The blood. It was all over my wrist. I had wiped it off after I killed him. But it was still there. Alfred's blood."

"But you just said you wiped it off."

"But it was still there, even if no one could see it. You didn't see it when you came, Claudine. I thought at least you would notice it, that you would help me get rid of it. But you didn't see it either! You just left me."

"Oh, Giulia darling, I didn't know, my poor baby."

"And I couldn't sleep, couldn't eat. I couldn't even bear to see Michael. He was so upset about Alfred. But why was he grieving so? Didn't he see what Alfred was? What he did? The blood? *My blood on his hands, his blood on mine.* He was the cancer. Don't you see? I had to cut it out. I had to stop him. Stop. Had to, had to, had. . ."

"Ralph, it's enough," Claudine said. "I am afraid Giulia cannot be allowed to go on like this." She motioned toward the nurse standing by with a hypodermic.

Approaching the bedside, the nurse briefly leaned over the agitated girl as Doctor Ingersoll held her fast and firmly, with a soothing touch and a gentle voice.

As Giuliana's own voice relaxed into near silence, her eyes became fixed on Claudine's familiar and comforting face. Pale and pathetic, the younger woman whispered a faintly audible, "Zia Claudia," as her eyes glazed over, drowned in sleep.

Amber rays poured through the western windows of the hospital room, strained through narrowed venetian blinds.

"She's got to rest now," Claudine said, "Ralph, I know you must understand. She has simply been through too much to continue at this point."

Ralph nodded as he turned off the tape recorder. It was always good to get a confession. But this was one of the few times he'd wished he'd gotten it from someone else.

EPILOGUE

He was wrapped tightly around her. He could feel her warm, silky, supple touch against his chest and cheek. Her hair tickled his nose. It felt so good after all those many months of bleak solitude. After all the death and the disillusionment, here was goodness. Claudine Ingersoll is goodness. She seems to purr with pleasure in his arms. If only it could stay like this without any interruption.

Oh no! Not the clock radio, not now.

Ring, ring!

No music?

Ring, ring!

Ralph reached over to shut it off, but it was the telephone ringing. Custer, startled by the noise and the bouncing mattress, yowled as he wrestled free from the place where he'd been sleeping, comfortably nestled up against Ralph's chest and tucked in under his chin.

"Hello," Ralph sputtered.

"Ralph? Sorry to wake you."

"How are you, Claudine?"

The dream. It had been too good to be true. The truth was that she was on the phone, it was ten o'clock on a mild September morning, and now even the damn cat had left him.

"I'm well. And you."

"O.K. How about Giuliana?"

"She is very much improved. She's even been able to speak to her lawyer, to cooperate in her own defense. We are hopeful now that, under the extenuating circumstances, the trial will be just, and Giulia will be able to recover with time."

"That *is* good news."

"Yes. But that is not why I called you."

After a pause she confessed.

"Ralph, I've been thinking of you these past two weeks. I actually find myself missing you, and I was wondering, could we have lunch together this afternoon at my place?"

"Nothing I'd rather do," Ralph replied with enthusiasm." In fact, I have been wanting to call you. Not just about the case, but about us, that is if there's an actual 'us' outside what we did together last month. For me there's no question about it. When I answered the phone and heard your voice on the other end of the line, I was . . . well, as a matter of fact, you may find this hard to believe, but you have just made my wildest dream come true."

The End

ABOUT THE AUTHOR

For over three decades, Judith Mitrani, PhD was a Training and Supervising Analyst at The Psychoanalytic Center of California. She was honored with Emeritus status when she retired from her clinical practice at the end of 2015. A Fellow of the International Psycho-Analytical Association, Dr. Mitrani's clinical/theoretical work has been published in nine languages. She is the author of many papers published in both American and international peer-reviewed journals, as well as the books *Framework for the Imaginary: Clinical Explorations in Primitive States of Being* (first published in 1996, and re-issued by Karnac in 2008), *Ordinary People and Extra-Ordinary Protections: a post-Kleinian Approach to the Treatment of Primitive Mental States* (New Library of Psychoanalysis, Routledge, 2000), *Taking The Transference: Essays on Psychoanalytic Technique* (Karnac, 2014) and the personal memoir, *The Most Beautiful Place in the World, a memoir of an Psychoanalyst and the Realization of a State of Mind* (2021). She is also co-editor of *Encounters with Autistic States: A Memorial Tribute to Frances Tustin* (Jason Aronson, 1997) and *Frances Tustin Today* (New Library of Psychoanalysis, Routledge, 2015) with her analyst/husband Dr. Theodore Mitrani. Judith Mitrani was the founding Chair of the Frances Tustin Memorial Trust, serving from 1995 until 2018, and she still supervises and lectures internationally on psychoanalytic technique. Since her retirement in Los Angeles in 2016, she has become a resident of Paris, France with her husband and her tabby cat Mickey.

Judith L. Mitrani, PhD

ACKNOWLEDGEMENTS

I wish to express my everlasting gratitude to Theodore Mitrani, my steadfast husband who not only saw me through the conception of this novel nearly 30-years ago, but has been by my side and in the mystery of how the story would develop during its gestation; To Liz Dubelman, a true friend whose constancy of encouragement, ideas, and thoughtful "checking in" at every turn were the acts of a true literary 'doula'; And to the wise and witty Ellis Weiner, whose editorial elegance and experience gave this project and me a leg up that was needed so that I might arrive at the finished line. I also extend my sincere thanks to Alex and Karl, who provided their 'PublishingPush' to find a place for this book in the overcrowded world of newborn fiction.

9 781802 272260